Twentieth-Century

Leatherman

an argument
a history
a love story

Drew D. Kramer

Twentieth-Century

Leatherman

an argument
a history
a love story

by Drew D. Kramer

Fair Page Media LLC
Springfield, PA

ISBN: 978-0-9989098-6-8

What Leaders of the Community are Saying about *Twentieth-Century Leatherman*

Gay men's leather culture evolved as a direct reaction to the oppression of gay men, which criminalized our sex. From hankies to runs to dark rooms gay men invented a culture that thrived away from and hidden to not only straight people but even most gays. Twentieth-century leathermen found a way to not only survive but to thrive in a time and county that hated them. The secrecy and mystery sure added to the hotness of it all but as AIDS hit and most of our elders started to die so too did much of our history. Drew Kramer is now one of those elders. He is one of the few older gay leathermen that were there and survived. We are blessed to have him guide us through leather history simply by telling us some of his stories. Twentieth-Century Leatherman *is a must read for anyone who strives to understand our history and will be an instant classic.*

Geoff Millard, Mr. San Francisco Leather 2017

Drew Kramer has penned a very personal story that is also a myth, a sacred narrative that shaped the first generations of leathermen. The story of Ryan, an utter novice, who becomes Farley's slave in a single night of passion, is not for everyone. There is no negotiation and little regard for consent. Some readers will justify this as a fantasy, which does not demand the same precautions and boundaries as real life. But it is not fantasy. This is a story about real men, men who loved masculinity and the experience of claiming or being claimed by another man. The transcendence of this 20th-century style of BDSM came from existential risk: throwing yourself off a cliff to hopefully be taught how to fly. In this hidden world of intense encounters, you might have only seconds to decide whether the man who offered you his collar was strong and wise enough to catch you before you crashed to the canyon floor. Whether any given connection grew into slavery was, on some level, not the point. The point was having the courage to pit your nerve, muscles, and stamina against the strength and accuracy of a sadist who crafted an ordeal that held up a mirror to your deepest self.

This book is a powerful record of the development of a queer subculture that could not survive unscathed into the 21ˢᵗ century. Kramer documents the social changes begotten by AIDS, gay liberation, and the politicization of radical sex. But instead of relegating leathermen to the footnotes, this text celebrates the creation and evolution of our black leather style, etiquette, fraternity, and love. It is a romance, a memoir, and an open-ended question about where these values will lead us. (Hopefully, we need more from each other than yet another leather contest.) Like Geoff Mains' Urban Aborginals, *William Carney's* The Real Thing, *Jack Fritscher's* Leather Blues, *and John Preston's* Mister Benson, *this is a classic that is both a novel and a documentary.*

The ending may surprise you. For a writer who idealizes the past, Kramer is not afraid to face big changes in exactly who qualifies as a 21ˢᵗ-century leatherman. From one gloved hand to a kneeling boy's shoulder, we pass on our ability to bond with and uplift one another. Read this book and find out what "freedom" can mean.

Patrick Califia, author of *Macho Sluts* and *Sensuous Magic*

This is a superb first novel by leatherman and activist and artist Drew Kramer. It swings back and forth between its characters and their viewpoints. There is a lot of leathersex and bondage. It takes place in New York in the last quarter of the 20ᵗʰ century. The journey of love and discovery is a powerful ride and an easy, fun read. Lovely to be back in the Mineshaft again. I read it twice in a week and enjoyed it immensely both times. This is a great novel and I highly recommend it to all Leather/BDSM folks. Best novel I have read in years!

Peter Fiske, author of *My Leather Life: Early Years*

Our lives as leathermen are often misunderstood. For an outsider looking in, leather, kink, and BDSM can appear uncaring and cold. However, while our experiences are unique they often share a deep, intense connection unlike any other. Kramer's work brings to us a collection of stories that is deeply moving and exhilarating. His narrative allows us a rare glimpse into a near-religious euphoria that we witness on the page. Those who have experienced it will

recognize it immediately and revel in the memories of a nearly-gone era. Those who have not can appreciate a new level of understanding of the power and strength that spews from each encounter. They are stories that need to be remembered and shared, and give us pause to think about what we have lost and what we want our leather future to be.

Gary Wasdin, Director, Leather Archives and Museum

Twentieth-Century Leatherman evokes the gay male leather experience from the 1970s to 2019. It incorporates stories of the men and the Dom/sub activities of these decades in sexy detail. It also faces how AIDS affected this community and how leathermen evolved into the 21st century. A finely-tooled, moving, instructive novel, living up to its promise as argument, history, and love story; the book's central characters, Farley and Ryan, become our friends, lovers, and family. Their joys and travails are central to our own context, past and present. Their story is the living argument for how generatively two lovers, whatever the brand of their sexuality, can navigate life together. The writing gleams. Bravo for creating this gift to us!

Guy Kettelhack, author of *Dancing Around The Volcano*

Dedication

This book is dedicated to the Twentieth-Century Leathermen I knew and loved who will never get to read this book because they have gone to their reward. In particular I name John McConnell, Andrew Harwin, Michael Horowitz, and Ted Menten. This is your story more than mine, and I hope I haven't made a hash of the telling of it.

Table of Contents

Palm Springs, California • July, 2009

"Goodnight, gentlemen. Thank you for coming out," John called from behind the bar. The ten or eleven customers still hanging around in the first hours of a Thursday morning downed their beers and shuffled out. A thin guy who made an appearance to drink vodka and soda and shoot pool paused before he headed out the door and called to John, "You have one more of us, on the patio," he paused, smirked, "the General."

John knew who he meant.

The man didn't call himself "the General," but that was how he was referred to by almost everyone, because of his resemblance to the cartoon character who served as the mascot to a home air conditioning contractor in its advertising.

John would let the General be for a bit. His hand brushed upwards on the switches for the houselights; and the patio, darker than the main bar, was lit up like a stage set. There in the corner, slouching slightly, sat the massive old man, his eyes buried beneath the brim of his Muir cap, a cigar that had doubtless gone out between the forefinger and middle finger of one powerful, meaty hand.

The bar called itself a "Leather Levi cruise bar," but, John reflected, the only toehold it had on being a leather bar was the few men like the General. Always in their black, gleaming leathers, wearing their heavy Langlitz or Schott jackets whenever the temperature at night went below ninety. True to form, John took in the General's black Wesco boots, his black leather chaps over worn blue jeans, black t-shirt stretched over his mass, and the face of a mustached sphinx beneath the Muir cap.

After scrutinizing him to make sure the old man wasn't dead, gone to whatever Leather Valhalla awaited him and his kind, John decided to let him doze a little longer. He moved pensively around the bar, wondering about who that man was, and who those few remaining Twentieth-Century leathermen were.

He recalled the history of young men plucked from farms and ranches in Wyoming and Ohio and Louisiana and North Dakota to serve in the Second World War, and there, in barracks and on troop ships, they found that they were not, in fact, the only ones. After the war, they stayed in those cities where the military had left them: New York, Los Angeles, and San Francisco, to make a new life for themselves. They bought motorcycles to get to and from whatever jobs they could find and would spend Sunday afternoons exploring these new cities on their bikes. Then Marlon Brando changed everything — rolling into town on a bike just like theirs, filling up the screen with his boots and leather jacket and swaggering with his hips slightly thrust forward so that the bulge in his jeans entered the room just before the rest of him. He was the man those young, lonely men desired, and so they imitated him. And then, out on one of those rides, stopping for a beer to wash the dust from their throats, they saw another young man ride up on his bike dressed similarly. There was barely a need for an introduction. The leather communicated everything that each man needed to know about the other.

In a world where one man knowing another was a "homosexual" gave him the power to destroy the deviant's life with one anonymous letter to an employer or the local chief of police, leather and boots provided a means to convey, "You are safe with me. I know what you want. I want that, too."

The glasses were all washed and replaced on the shelves, the beer coolers were stocked; it was time.

John swung open the door to the patio.

"Excuse me…" he mumbled, and then checked himself.

"Sir!" he began again, with a note of deference in his voice, and stepped through the door.

The old man roused, hearing himself so addressed. He opened his eyes and saw a backlit silhouette of a man, and in his bourbon bleariness, that outline was familiar, one he remembered from long ago.

"Boy!" he said. John heard a note of panic and bewilderment. "Boy! It's you. Ryan… I prayed for you, boy. I prayed for you…"

New York City • May, 1980

"It's just a bar," Ryan told himself. "It's just a bar." He would go in, order a beer, and drink his beer, and that would be it. He didn't even need to finish the beer. He could spend a few hours in a diner and then head to the Port Authority Bus Terminal and sleep in one of the hard plastic potato-chip chairs until the first bus in the morning if this adventure proved to be a bust. Anyway, he was feeling the temperature drop, and it would be warm in the bar.

Two men made up his mind for him. They brushed past him and pushed open the door, the last of the pair paused, planted his black leather boot to prop open the door, turned, and said to Ryan, "Coming in, stud?"

"Yeah, thanks," said Ryan, and followed them.

"Stud. Huh." That was a first.

Ryan moved slowly, entering the bar as one does wading into a river for a midnight swim. Eyes met his and he looked away. He picked out the bartender, shirtless and muscular, and made his way towards him. Across the bar he ordered a Rolling Rock, from Pennsylvania, just like he was.

"How you doing tonight?" the bartender asked.

"Pretty good," Ryan answered, trying to sound confident, passing dollars across the bar.

Beer in hand, he turned. Other than the bare bulb hanging over the cash register, the only light in the bar was over the pool table.

Just outside of that circle of light, Ryan's eyes were drawn to a dark form. He wasn't sure if there was a man there at all — just a patch of the darkness that appeared somehow darker than the gloom that surrounded it. The hairs on the back of Ryan's neck stood on end, the same sensation that an antelope feels when the stealthy cougar silently moves itself within striking distance.

Ryan dug in the pocket of his jeans and pulled out a box of Marlboros and a Bic lighter. He drew one from the box, raised it to his lips, lit it, and inhaled deeply. At that same moment he saw the cherry red end of a cigar head high in the blacker than black form glow like a beacon. Ryan moved towards the place where the glow had been.

As Ryan got closer, his eyes distinguished the man from the black paint on the wall behind him. It was like some deep buried erotic fantasy manifesting itself in flesh and black leather, like some ancient demon becoming corporeal out of the darkness. The cigar was now stuck in the man's jaw, and beneath a thick, black mustache, Ryan was sure he saw a smile. It was his impression that it was a smile of satisfaction.

Ryan stopped, unsure of what to do next, sensing that speaking first would be somehow stepping out of line. The man's eyes were invisible beneath the shining brim of the leather hat he wore. Ryan's eyes dropped to the man's black boots.

"Well boy," the man growled, "aren't you going to introduce yourself? Let's have your name, boy."

The man at the door addressing him as "stud" had sounded awkward, but being addressed as "boy" didn't give Ryan a moment's pause, as though he had never had another name.

"... and you address me as "Sir" or you will be sorry you didn't, boy."

"Ryan, Sir. My name is Ryan. Sir."

"Good boy," said the man. "Come closer, Ryan." The man expelled a billow of cigar smoke and in coming closer, Ryan moved into it.

When Ryan was close enough to feel the man's body heat, he halted his advance. His eyes again dropped to the man's boots, uncomfortable in the knowledge that he was being surveyed.

The man's gloved right hand went to Ryan's left pectoral muscle and sat there, as though feeling Ryan's heart beat. More smoke burned Ryan's eyes.

"You're a sturdy young man, aren't you," the man said, "I bet you can take a lot."

"Yes Sir," Ryan answered.

Ryan remembered the cigaret in his hand. He put it to his mouth and hauled deeply on it. He held the smoke for a moment, then exhaled it out of the side of his mouth. He smiled, "I bet I can, Sir."

"You're coming home with me, boy."

The man's left hand took the cigar from his mouth, another plume of smoke enveloped Ryan; the right hand moved from his chest to the back of Ryan's neck and then drew Ryan closer. Their mouths were millimeters apart; Ryan felt the bristle of the mustache on his lips. Weak in the knees, he shifted his weight forward slightly against the man, smelling the acrid breath, the leather, the man's musk. The man pressed Ryan still closer, and Ryan relaxed against the solidity of the leather-clad stranger. He suddenly felt much younger than his nineteen years. He was a child, frightened by something nameless, suddenly safe in the arms of his powerful father.

Safe. That was it. He felt safe. Pressed against this powerful man whose name he didn't even know, he felt safe, safer than he had ever felt. Cared for and watched over. So safe.

"Oh Sir..." Ryan whispered, "Thank you, Sir..."

"Let's go, boy," said the man.

Again the gloved hand was at the back of Ryan's neck. "Turn around, boy," came the order. Ryan allowed himself to be pivoted where he stood. Another command: "Head down. Hands behind your back."

Ryan complied.

He felt cold, hard steel at his left wrist, then slightly-applied pressure, and a click; and the handcuff encircled his left wrist. Ryan became aware that his dick was hard as iron pipe. The process, unseen, was repeated with his right wrist.

"Move."

Ryan was gently but firmly propelled through the dark bar. At the door, he stopped as the man stepped even with him, pushed open the door, and guided Ryan out onto the sidewalk.

The man stepped in front of Ryan and raised his arm to signal a cab. For the first time Ryan saw him in the streetlights. The man was about two inches shorter than Ryan, so five foot, ten inches or so, but he must outweigh him by fifty or sixty pounds. His shoulders were massive, straining the seams of the black leather jacket he wore. His thighs seemed to be the girth of Ryan's waist. A yellow taxi eased to the curb. The man opened the door and beckoned to Ryan, smiling that same smile of satisfaction. As Ryan bowed his head to clamber into the back seat of the cab, the man put his hand on the back of Ryan's head. Ryan was reminded of the same gesture he had seen on cop shows, the suspect being loaded into the back of a patrol car.

Once in, the man slammed the door closed, came around the back of the car, and climbed in the other side.

"Good evening, Sir! How are you tonight, Sir! Where are we going, Sir?" asked the turbaned driver.

The man gave an address on West 80th Street and they were off. Ryan glanced out the window at the dark buildings they were passing, homeless people here and there, men dressed in leather, headed to the bar they had just left. Then he turned to turned to the man, his abductor.

The man arched his back and his hands worked the buttons on his jeans; then the man extracted a fat dick and balls the size of eggs from their package. "Get your mouth on that dick, boy," the man ordered.

His hands cuffed behind him, Ryan bent forward, and for the first time in his life tasted the salt and tang of cock. He started working his mouth on it like it was an ice cream cone, opening wide, letting his tongue explore. The taxi stopped at a light, paused, then shot off again. The man gave a growl of pleasure. Ryan could sense the man's dick getting fatter and firmer. He worked harder, getting it slick with his spit. The man's cock was now standing at attention. "Now swallow that dick, boy."

Ryan did as told. But his throat revolted. He heaved. "Try again, keep breathing through your nose. You just relax and let it happen, boy. You're going to spend a lot of time sucking that dick, so you better learn to like doing it."

Ryan steeled himself. He took a deep breath through his nose and slowly lowered his head, letting the man's dick bury itself in his mouth. When the man's member hit the back of his throat, Ryan made himself relax, another breath, and this time he felt his throat soften and welcome the intruder. He eased off a bit, working his tongue, then lowered his mouth again.

"Good boy! I'm impressed!" growled the man. "Just like that. Up and down, and taking it all every time."

Ryan's mind went blank. He lost himself in sucking cock. Nothing seemed more natural. His pace was relaxed, almost lazy.

"Ease up for now," said the man, and then to the driver: "Middle of the block, pull up next to that white Cadillac."

The man drew a wallet on a heavy chrome-plated chain from his back pocket, pulled out a ten, passed it to the driver, and said, "Two dollars back."

"Sir! Thank you very much, Sir! You gentlemen have a good evening!"

The man got out of the cab, his stiff dick and balls bobbing in the cool springtime night. He came around and opened the door for handcuffed Ryan, who lumbered to his feet. Again the hand at the nape of Ryan's neck, and the man guided him up the stairs of a brownstone. The man's left hand unclipped the keys from where they hung from his belt and unlocked the door. They climbed a flight of ancient wooden stairs, again keys were fitted into a lock, and a door swung open. "You stay there, boy," commanded the man.

The man entered, the door closed behind him, leaving Ryan in the hallway. He heard movement behind the door, then silence.

Ryan's knees began to buckle slightly. For the first time he didn't feel safe. He remembered that not a soul in the world knew where he was. Again sounds of movement behind the door, the stomp of approaching boots; the door swung open.

The man stepped behind Ryan. "Open your dick-sucking mouth, boy."

Ryan obeyed.

Hands came around in front, holding something black and leathery. A form like a bag lifted in front of him held by both hands, the bottom of the opening caught on Ryan's upper deck of teeth, and the leather bag went over his head. Then, the portion of the bag in his mouth was pulled down over his chin. With the pulling of a cord laced at the back, the leather tightened around his head. Not a bag — it was a hood.

Ryan was sightless. The sounds that reached his ears were now slightly muffled. There was, however, an opening for his mouth. His dick-sucking mouth, the man had called it. The laced cord tightened, a buckle was closed at the base of his skull. Now more sensation: padded leather encircled Ryan's neck, another buckle at the back. Ryan's left leg began to quaver as an image of himself, hooded and collared and handcuffed, arose in his mind's eye. A new sound, a clip being applied beneath his chin, then a tug forward. He was at the end of a leash. Leashed and collared. The command was wordless. Again Ryan obeyed, being led blindly into the man's apartment.

Step. Step. Step. Step. Step. Then brought up short. The left leg again. Ryan again felt the heft of the man's body, heard the creak of his leathers, albeit muffled by the hood. The man's bulk enfolded Ryan. Ryan relaxed. He heard himself whimper. Again this profound feeling of safety. He was safe in this powerful man's arms. Safe as he had never felt himself to be before.

"I own you now, boy. You're my property. And starting tonight I am going to enjoy the hell out of my property."

"Yes Sir," said Ryan.

The man separated himself and again Ryan felt himself guided forward by a tug on the leash. Now his steps were not so tentative; he could trust the man. A hand to the chest told him to stop, and the leash was draped over his shoulder. Fumbling with the handcuffs and they were removed. His arms felt awkward at his sides, so Ryan replaced them behind his back, wrist to wrist. The hands, caressing him gently, moved to his belt, unbuckled it, unbuttoned his jeans, unzipped the zipper, and took out Ryan's dick and balls, handling them as though they were fragile. Ryan became aware that his dick was soft, but with the sensation of the leather gloves moving over the shaft and cupping his balls, that quickly changed. His jeans were tugged down until they bound his ankles.

Next he felt his leather bar vest being removed. Ryan had only bought it that afternoon. The previous Saturday he had passed the store on Christopher Street four times, once going all the way around the block. (He didn't know that the man in the store had noticed his hesitation on the first approach before his resolve evaporated and moved on, and had smiled.) The fifth attempt brought conviction. He entered the store and stood stunned by what he saw: the walls covered completely from floor to ceiling in black leather. The smell of the place was almost overpowering. After the perfunctory exchange, Ryan had been taken in hand. Charles' hands were capable indeed. He had a decade of experience in retail and knew the tricks of the trade, complimenting people on their choices of what to wear as they walked in the door, starting off with something he knew they would not like at the outset so when he unveiled something that they did like it was like uncovering the Holy Grail… But, at the Leatherman NYC, he kept these tools of the trade zipped up in his tool bag. Here he had more important work to do than moving merchandise.

After a few tokes, he might explain, stumbling over his words

before he got going, that he considered his work something of a sacred calling. "Put on the full armor of God" was often the text taken for sermons in the Baptist Church that loomed so large in his childhood. And that was what he was doing: preparing these men for battle. Leather is battle gear for warriors of love. It was Charles' job to make sure their loins were well girded. The leather jockstraps and codpieces were not just covering for decency's sake but became the focal point. The harness accentuated the parts of the upper body—the breadth of the shoulders, the meatiness of the pecs, the swell of the triceps—while distracting from those that were less than assets.

But Charles loved this experience, when a man whose very sweat carried a whiff of fear and ambivalence of what he was getting himself into was propelled through the door by desires he did not understand. And there was Charles waiting for him, waiting to strip him bare, have him shed the clothes that would no longer serve him, then by the magic of tanned cowhide adorn him how he was meant to be adorned. Charles would position his pilgrim seekers with their backs to the full length mirror until the process was complete, then turn them around, watching their faces as they got a first look at the stranger who had been walking in their footsteps all along.

He explained to him that being fitted for a vest was not a simple thing. The cut and the draping had to show off his body in just the right way. It had to fall to just above where his belt sat, showing a horizontal ribbon of the skin of his back. And, with his belt opened up a notch, his jeans now sat lower, so that the very top of his butt crack peaked over.

Ryan's eyes had fallen to his Adidas sneakers, which now seemed like a party balloon at some midsummer pagan rite — completely out of place. Charles' eyes followed Ryan's and the talk turned to the virtues of Redwing boots. Ryan's feet slipped inside. They were as comfortable as bedroom slippers.

Ryan surveyed himself in the mirror. Six foot even, shaggy blond hair in a mop on his head. Naturally athletic, he had made the varsity baseball team in high school and was one of the better sprinters on the track team. He had started shaving his sophomore year, and blond chest hair adorned his well-developed chest. "Christ," Charles had said over Ryan's shoulder, "you're gonna make out, man."

Ryan had drifted through high school, working only as hard as he had to in order to keep his grades as high as his coaches required. He didn't enjoy school, and passed on college prep courses. After graduation he had gone to the local community college, starting with taking classes in business. His father ran a hardware store and had found a job for Ryan. For no other reason than he thought it would be easy, he took a theater class in his first semester at college. The first assignment was to memorize a soliloquy. The teacher, Ms. Bender, had guided him to Tom's speech at the end of *The Glass Menagerie*. The other students had fumbled or hammed their way through in turn, but Ryan brought the house down, earning him his first round of applause. The first summer after college he got the part of Vladimir in a local theater troop's production of *Waiting For Godot*. Ms. Bender demanded that he start classes with an actor's workshop in New York City, and for the past six months, every Saturday, he had taken the bus up and spent Saturdays "mastering the craft" as the other aspiring actors described it.

Ryan had known since he was thirteen that he was attracted to men rather than to the girls in his class. He took this in stride, but kept the information to himself. Although opportunities had presented themselves in the form of his high school biology lab partner, a quiet, gawky boy, and recently, one of his fellow acting students, all these seemed to be missing the mark. He beat off thinking about Mr. Dennis, his gym teacher, with his brush cut and military bearing, and Ollie, who worked at his father's hardware store and who had gotten Ryan started on smoking. Overhearing the conversation of two of his more obviously gay aspiring actors after class on 38th Street, he would walk south to the West Village before taking the subway up to Port Authority to catch a later bus back home. Skulking the streets, he had seen men who he was interested in, and had come across the store that seemed to have called to him. Noticing two men wearing chaps exit, he had felt compelled to visit.

Swallowing hard, Ryan raised the topic of price for the boots and the vest. It was not as much as he feared it would be, but it was more than he had, about twice the amount of his paycheck from the hardware store. He asked Charles if he could hold the vest and the boots until next week. "I'll be here and so will they," he was assured. On his way out, he did have enough money to buy a copy of a magazine. Although it was called *Drummer*, it didn't have anything to do with drumming.

On the bus ride home, he read it cover to cover. The lyrics of John Denver's "Rocky Mountain High" summed up how the stories and photos and illustrations in the magazine made him feel: it was like coming home again to a place he'd never been. There it was. It was all there. How could it be that these longings and desires buried so deep down he couldn't express them in words were not his alone, but were shared by many, many men? So many that in the back pages were listings of bars and clubs, and apparently these men had their act together enough to publish an actual magazine, just like the *Time* magazines that were piled in a rack next to the toilet in the bathroom he shared with his father. The longing in the eyes of one man in the magazine became Ryan's longing. The man, stripped almost naked save for his boots, was on his knees, looking up at a man whose face was impassive, almost indifferent. In the intervening week Ryan read and re-read the magazine, distracted at school and at work. The store on Christopher Street was a gateway to a world where he belonged, and the price of passage was the cost of the boots and the vest.

He told his father that he needed money for an additional class at the school in New York City. This was one of the only lies he had ever told to his father, who valued honesty above all else and who had fired a longtime employee when he caught the man in a lie. His father agreed, but would dock his son's check by twenty dollars every payday until the debt was paid off.

The next Saturday had been warm. Wearing only a t-shirt and jeans, Ryan had made an excuse and left his acting class early, so urgent was the beckoning. He asked the man at the store about a bar he found listed in the back of *Drummer* magazine.

"Going to the Eagle tonight to show these off?" Charles asked.

"Yeah, maybe, but I don't live here. I don't have anywhere to stay tonight and the last bus is at 10:05."

"Looking like that, you don't have to worry about where you're staying tonight."

And so, when the man who brought him home from the bar slowly removed Ryan's vest, it left Ryan feeling more than naked. He felt unmanned and powerless. Like some medieval knight stripped of his armor. The vest was the emblem of his budding identity. Without it, who and what was he?

Transfixed by the vest, he barely noticed as his shirt was removed.

Ryan stood naked and hooded, but not for long.

Two hands pushed him at the hips backwards. He fell and found himself sitting. The piece of furniture was firm but padded, but his bare ass recognized that he was sitting on leather.

Another command. "Off with the boots, then shuck your pants and jockey shorts, then back on with the boots."

Ryan complied, fumbling blindly.

"Now on your knees, boy."

Ryan eased off his perch and dropped to his knees, grateful that the floor was carpeted. He found his face buried in the man's crotch. "You know what to do."

Ryan's dick-sucking mouth sucked the man's dick.

The man started talking, low and gruff, barely above a whisper. Ryan had to strain his ears as the sound was muffled by the tight leather hood.

"Some men are born to be served by other men. Some men are born to serve — only finding satisfaction and contentment in obedience and submission. You are one of those men. You will serve me. Your only pleasure will be giving me pleasure. Your dick is off limits from now on. You do not touch it without my permission. Even when you piss. The only dick you need to be concerned with is the one you're sucking."

And then, closer to his ear, "and another thing that gives me pleasure. Gives me great pleasure. Know what that is? Hurting you."

With this new information Ryan paused.

"Did I tell you to stop, boy?"

"No, Sir!" gulped Ryan unintelligibly, his mouth full of fat cock.

"That's it. All the way up and all the way down. And keep that tongue busy on the shaft."

Ryan redoubled his efforts. Again, as in the taxi, he cleared his mind, let his mouth and throat do what they were quickly learning how to do.

Suddenly, the man pulled out.

Again the voice, guttural, growling, close to his ear, "Are you ready to hurt for me, boy?"

"Yes, Sir," Ryan replied, barely audibly.

"On your feet, slave."

Ryan struggled to his feet. Again, Ryan's left leg began to shake, betraying his fear.

"Behind you is a bed. Lie down and stretch out on it. On your belly, boy."

Ryan stepped slowly backwards. Against the back of his knees he felt what he now knew to be a bed, covered in leather. He shifted his weight and sat down, then slowly eased himself back until his booted feet were just over the edge. He flopped over on his belly.

Ryan sensed movement. The man's hands took his hips and shifted Ryan to the left. Then, taking each foot by the heel of the boot, Ryan's feet were spread apart. Ryan bit his lip and took a deep breath through his nose, inhaling the smell of the leather hood that tightly encased his head. The smell seemed to ease his mind, slowing down the apprehensive thoughts and the images that cascaded through his consciousness.

Ryan felt bands being wound around his booted ankles and then tied off.

Next, the process was repeated with Ryan's wrists. His bonds, now that he wasn't feeling them through his boots, were

straps of soft leather, about an inch and a half wide. When these were tied off, arms and legs outstretched, he was all but immobilized, only able to flex his muscles, extend his fingers, and crane his neck.

He thought he heard an appreciative noise from the man.

Then movement from behind him: the mattress sank, and the man crawled on top of him. The gloved hands caressed his legs, then his butt, his back, his outstretched arms. The man lay on top of him. Ryan struggled to fill his lungs with the weight compressing his chest. He felt the stubble of the man's chin and the bristle of his mustache abrade his shoulders. The man relaxed his hips, and his meaty dick nestled in the crack of Ryan's ass.

The man's bulk gave Ryan courage. Again, the feeling of safety. Ryan felt he was ready for whatever came next.

"Nothing for you to do but take it, boy. Make all the noise you want. The neighbors are used to it."

The man rolled off Ryan; the mattress rebounded as he got off the bed.

Ryan breathed deeply. Time seemed to have stopped.

The silence was broken by a slapping sound. Then Ryan felt heat in his buttocks. He remembered the man's thick, black leather belt. A pause, then another blow. Harder this time. And then another, still harder.

A sound escaped Ryan's lips: "Aww…"

"All the noise you want," the man repeated.

And then another crack of the belt. And another. And another. The blows came faster and harder, building imperceptibly. The sting from the individual strikes seemed to blend together. Ryan felt intense heat from his ass, like sitting on a flagstone made blazing hot by the sun at the local public pool. Hotter and hotter, the cracks of the belt on his ass were now staccato. "JEEZUSSS" moaned Ryan. The belt was relentless. From deep inside Ryan grew a growl that exploded out of him in a bellow. It repeated itself, like someone depressing a key on an organ and a deep, low note sounding from the pipes, then letting up, then pressed down again, then letting up, then pressed down again, getting louder and louder. "Unnhh... UNNNHHH..!"

Ryan ceased to be human, or if still human, some much more primitive man was created under the man's belt. He growled. More bellowing. He gnashed his teeth.

Then, suddenly, it ceased.

Ryan was panting, still making his groaning, growling noises. His breathing slowed and he choked down a few good drafts of air, filling his chest.

Crack.

The belt fell again. This time, across Ryan's shoulders. "Agh!" he cried out at the change in location. He had been gulled into thinking that the ordeal was over. He felt himself begin to panic at this new assault.

"Breathe deep, boy. Just take what's coming. I'm nowhere near done with you."

Ryan drew a deep breath. "Fuck," he told himself, "I can take this."

Another crack of the belt on his upper back, and then again the growing heat as the blows rained down. Now there was no holding back. Ryan abandoned himself to the experience.

From some remote crevice of his consciousness he heard himself laughing, or crying, or some response to the whipping that was both and neither. Hot tears stung his cheeks and the leather-sheathed mattress was soon wet with them.

Then, suddenly, it stopped. Ryan arched his back and flexed his muscles, sucking and expelling air in and out between his clenched teeth. Again, the feeling that time had stopped, he was bound spread-eagle on some distant, empty planet, the surface smooth as a billiard ball except for him. The outlines of his body became indistinct to him; they seemed to expand and contract, drifting, radiating from the pools of heat on his back and his butt.

Then, suddenly, the most gentle caress, just with the fingertips, just touching the so-fine-as-to-be-invisible blond hairs on Ryan's back. Ryan whimpered and then he wailed. He exploded in sobs and weeping, broken completely. The recollection of the physical pain vanished, replaced by something deeper, some great grief and longing, and fear too great for any one man to contain, beyond the experiences of his young life, but rather drawing from a source inherited from his father, and which his father had inherited from his father, going back and back and back to when some ancient ancestor looked out over a grassy savannah where a terrible battle had taken place and realized that all his brothers lay dead around him. Ryan felt sanity leave him as he descended down and down and down into this bottomless chasm, forsaken and lost.

The gentle touch became firmer. The outstretched hand pressed into the quivering muscles of Ryan's back. Through the leather glove strength seemed to flow into Ryan. The sobbing subsided, the young man gasped for air. The growling voice in his ear whispered, "You are magnificent. You are precious beyond rubies, outshining the stars, you are golden. You are mine forever."

Ryan, bound and helpless, now felt powerful as he had never felt powerful before. He had come through. He had taken it. This man, this incredible man, had uncovered within him a strength he did not guess he had. Never before had Ryan felt more alive, and more "Ryan," more who he was and who he was meant to be.

"Sir…" he whispered, "Thank you, Sir."

The man chuckled.

"Oh. guaranteed. You're going to thank me alright, boy."

"Yes, Sir. Yes, Sir. Whatever I have to give is yours, Sir. Thank you, Sir."

The man's hand gently and slowly moved down Ryan's back, following his spine, and traced and retraced the crack of Ryan's ass. One gloved finger then wedged its way between his ass cheeks and the tip came to rest on Ryan's asshole. Ryan let out a little groan. The finger tip pressed slightly more firmly, then started to swirl and twist.

"Sir…" said Ryan gravely, "I've never done that before."

The finger was removed.

"Are you saying…?" asked the man, stunned.

"I've never done any of this before, Sir. Any of it."

"Are you saying," the man began again, "that I'm about to fuck your cherry ass?"

The wording made Ryan giggle.

"Yes, Sir. That's what I'm saying, Sir."

"Well," said the man, "now I'm really gonna enjoy this. You

probably aren't. It hurts 'til you get used to it, 'til I train your hole, but I sure am. You're gonna be begging for it before too long, but tonight you're gonna be begging me to stop. So just beg away."

Ryan swallowed hard.

"Yes, Sir," he said.

The next sensation Ryan felt was the finger again, poking at his hole, but the sensation was different. It felt moist and cold. His ass hole clenched like a fist. The man's finger probed deeper and seemed to slide. Ryan realized he had applied some kind of grease. The finger moved away, then returned, this time with a dollop of the stuff. The finger probed again and pressed a little deeper, then withdrew, then probed again, deeper still. Ryan's muscles relaxed. He inhaled deeply and slowly exhaled. The finger was now gliding in and out of his hole, gently twisting and turning, opening him up. Then two fingers. Ryan focused on relaxing all his muscles. Two fingers became three. Soon they were extending as far into Ryan as they would go.

The sensation was entirely new. Ryan was intrigued by the novelty. This subtle but firmly-applied pressure. Then, when the three fingers were buried as far as they would go, Ryan felt the fingertips wiggle slightly. Electricity seemed to suddenly flow from the fingertips to a point at the root of his cock and from there radiate outwards. His cock became engorged and Ryan moaned.

"Yeah," the man said, "you're ready as you'll ever be."

The finger was withdrawn. Ryan continued to breath deeply.

"Yeah, boy..." Ryan heard the man say.

A command: "Raise your butt as far up off the mattress as you can, boy."

Ryan obeyed. He felt a pillow shoved underneath his pelvis.

The man's weight compressed the mattress at the foot of the bed.

"Here it comes," thought Ryan.

The man pushed Ryan's knees further apart; Ryan adjusted to this new position.

"Arch your back, boy."

Ryan felt his butt cheeks being spread apart; then the warmth of what he knew to be the man's dick slid slowly up and down in the crack of his ass as the finger had done at the outset, stopping at the hole and lingering there, then feeling pressure.

Ryan felt his hole contract again. He redoubled his efforts at deep breathing.

"Clench and hold, then release. Clench and hold, then release. Keep doing that."

Ryan grunted a little as he clenched his asshole for all he was worth. Then, exhaling, relaxed. After a few repetitions, he again felt the head of the man's dick against his rosebud. Now, with each relaxation, slightly more pressure. Ryan felt his hole opening up to received the man's cock. He was going to get fucked.

Suddenly, with the relaxing and the exhalation came a thrust. The man's fat dick plunged into him.

The pain was ferocious. "Take it out! Take it out! Please, Sir! Take it out! It hurts!"

"Told you it would hurt. Now that I'm in, I'm gonna ride you 'till I shoot, boy!"

The pain diminished but only slightly. Ryan's hole fought against accommodating the man's rock hard member. A slight withdrawal, then another thrust.

"Oh fuck oh fuck oh fuck…" sang Ryan.

"Yeah boy, I'm fucking you now."

In and out, in and out. Relentless.

"Push back when I'm going in, boy"

Ryan complied. He focused on maintaining the rhythm that the man established. The pace quickened. Again, although more intense this time, Ryan felt that electricity. He found that by arching his back, the man's dick seemed to be hitting some heretofore unknown switch. Neither painful nor quite pleasurable, he felt his own dick getting harder. Now, when the man thrust in him, Ryan met the thrust by pushing his hips back with equal force. The mans hips were now slapping against Ryan's belt-tenderized ass. Ryan laughed. "Oh fuck, fuck me, Sir!"

"Oh yeah boy! This is your first fuck but it's not gonna be your last!"

Ryan was not aware of his toes curling, but the electricity seemed to flow from what he would learn was his prostate out into his limbs, and then he slowly felt the energy returning. From his outstretched arms and legs, closer and closer to the point of origin, the electric sensation flowed. When it hit home Ryan felt his body explode. His balls erupted. His load spattered on the leather mattress cover. "Oh fuck Sir!" he screamed, "Oh fuck!"

As Ryan's body collapsed helpless under him, the man increased his pace to jackhammer speed. Now it was the man's turn to let out a bellow—a bellow of conquest and domination—as he shot his seed deep into Ryan. Ryan felt everything, the batter racing down the shaft and then spattering inside him.

Still inside, still throbbing out his load, the man collapsed on top of Ryan, panting. Although wordless, the timber of the noises that the man made rose slightly in pitch. Ryan, astonished, realized that the man was crying. "Oh," said the man, and swallowed a sob. He pinned Ryan beneath him with his leather-clad bulk until both of their breathing, now in sync, returned to a normal rate. They lay together quietly until their sweat-drenched bodies felt the chill that comes with the evaporation. The man raised himself up and clambered off of Ryan. Ryan lay still as the man set about releasing Ryan from his bonds.

"Sit up, boy."

Ryan raised himself on his knees and elbows and pushed his torso up, sitting on the bed, his legs curled under him. He felt the man working the buckle of the hood, and then slowly, patiently, undoing the laces at the back of the hood. Pulled forward from the back, the hood peeled off. Even though the light in the room was dim, Ryan squinted and winced as his retinas adjusted.

He turned his head and looked at the man. If he had expected a smile he would have been disappointed, but he had not expected a smile. The man's face was as inscrutable as ever. The Muir cap removed, Ryan saw that his hair, jet black as his mustache, was worn in a sharp brush cut, looking like it was carved from onyx. The man still wore his leather jacket, boots, and leather gloves.

The man took two steps back and pointed with a thick forefinger at the floor in front of him. "Get your ass over here now, boy."

Ryan hustled to comply.

On his knees, looking up at the man, Ryan recalled the picture in *Drummer* magazine. He knew, though, that it was not an expression of yearning on his face. If he had glanced in the mirror, he would have seen awe and gratitude in his features. The man took his still semi-hard dick in one hand and put another again at the back of Ryan's head. "Put it in your mouth," he ordered.

A little surprised, Ryan opened wide and let the man's dick fill his mouth. He tasted the grease and found it vaguely familiar. (On the bedside table was a tub of Crisco.) He also tasted the tang of a few drops of come that seeped from the man's piss slit, and the *umami* of his own ass juices.

"Just take this, boy," the man said as he tilted back his head. He let out a deep sigh and Ryan felt his mouth flooded with the man's piss. A noise escaped him.

"Swallow, boy. Don't you spill one drop of the piss of the man who owns you."

Ryan swallowed, gulping down the hot liquid, not even noticing if he liked the taste or didn't, but thinking it tasted the way a bale of straw smells. The stream of piss weakened and then, after a few contractions, there were just a few final drops.

Now the man favored Ryan with a smile. Ryan felt his heartbeat quicken and his eyes begin to tear. He smiled up at the man.

"Now. Show me your appreciation of me using you as a urinal by licking my boots, boy."

Ryan bent over. He began by a light kiss to the toe. Then

another. Then he extended his tongue. He lapped at the boot leather. The taste of the man's piss was married to the taste of the man's boots in his mouth. "Mmmmm," the man purred. Ryan worked his way from the toe down the outside and as far around the back of the heel as he could. He noticed that leather has a taste to it, a unique taste. He came back to the toe, then returned to the heel on the inside. Taking his time, making sure his mouth hit every inch of the foot of the boot, he then switched to its fellow and repeated the process. When done, he slowly worked his tongue up the shaft, again taking care to do a thorough job. As with sucking the man's dick, Ryan lost himself in his labor; that shaft complete, he returned to the boot he had started with, addressing his attention to its shaft.

He rocked back and rested on his ankles, scrutinizing his work. Satisfied with his efforts, he looked up at the man. His face had returned to stern impassivity.

The man extended his hand palm upwards and raised it six inches. Ryan interpreted this as a signal to rise to his feet and did so. The man nodded then turned his back to him. He unbuckled the belt on his leather jacket and unzipped it. He dropped his arms to his side and relaxed his shoulders, then gave a quarter turn of his head. Ryan took hold of the jacket, pulled it over the man's shoulders, and then held it. The man turned back around and pointed to the closet. Ryan took the leather jacket and found an empty hanger. As he inserted the hanger he felt compelled to bury his face in the interior. He breathed deeply, taking in the man's smell. He hung the jacket in the closet.

The man sat down on the bed, looked pointedly at Ryan, and then down at his boots. Ryan crouched in front of the man. Again the feeling of peace and safety welled in him. He grabbed one boot by the heel and slowly wrenched it off. He raised the boot to his lips, then set it aside towards the foot of the bed. Then off with the second boot, another kiss, and it joined its fellow. The man pointed to Ryan's new Redwings, gave a nod, and then took off his own socks. Ryan, sitting on the floor which made the task a little awkward, took off his own boots and socks. He didn't think it would be right to stand them next to the man's boots, so he crawled over and set them at the side of the nightstand.

Ryan knelt at the man's feet, naked except for the padded leather collar he still wore. The man peeled off his gloves and gave a swat to Ryan's smiling face.

From a dresser drawer the man retrieved a quilt, which looked as if it had been made by some aunt or grandmother. His eyes caught the pool of Ryan's come on the leather mattress cover and frowned. He looked towards Ryan, snapped his fingers, and pointed to the patch of slickness. Ryan at first scanned the room for something to clean up his mess, but then, as if reading the man's mind, bent over the bed and sucked up his jism, then rubbed the smear of his saliva until it spread out and dried. He climbed back off the bed. The man tossed a few pillows retrieved from the floor onto the bed and spread out the quilt. He climbed into bed, got comfortable on his back, resting his head on the pillows, treated Ryan to the warmest smile yet, and invited Ryan to join him.

Ryan climbed beside the man. Although big and powerfully built himself, curled against the bulk and heft of the man, his head resting on the fur of his chest, Ryan felt small by comparison.

Lights out and the man was snoring almost immediately. Ryan tried to stay awake as long as he could, savoring the experience, fearful that it would all vanish with the dawn. Soon though, Ryan sank into deep and dreamless sleep.

New York City • October, 1973

"**A**nd did your mother offer any explanation or excuse for forgetting you at the market?" asked Doctor Solvang.

Farley Lustig pretended to consider the question. He took a long draw on his cigaret.

Farley thought of these sessions with his psychiatrist as a chess match. His boss at the Federal Reserve Bank of New York had been very firm when he made the suggestion and passed Doctor Solvang's card across the table to him.

This had followed an incident that disturbed everyone in the office. One of the secretaries, trying to heat mascara on the lightbulb on her desk lamp, had caused the bulb to pop. Farley, on his way to the men's room, was at that moment passing by her desk.

Suddenly, he was back in Viet Nam. At night bullets glow orange as they make their way through the darkness, singing as they go. Some nights the air was filled with these small fire demons and their song. Farley had cowered next to a filing cabinet, crying, his eyes wide as saucers. It was twenty minutes, he was told, before he composed himself. He assured everyone that he was perfectly alright and told them to get back to work. But his boss had thought it would be to everyone's benefit if he "saw a man about that" and said he knew a good one.

Doctor Solvang was a handsome Swede, about forty years old. After Farley had given the abridged version of his time in the jungles of Southeast Asia, Solvang continued to probe, sensing that there were more interesting things to talk about with this formal, stern man than shellshock.

"You have never married?" he had asked.

Farley explained that his job was a demanding one, and the hours he worked were long. Not only did that leave him little time to get out and about, but surely it would be unfair to give a wife long hours sitting alone at home even if he could find one to agree to such a proposition.

This of course was a lie. Farley invariably was at his desk at nine in the morning and his chair was empty by half past five at the latest. He was very good at his job, scheduling batches of data to be processed by the computer. He never erred in his calculations, as reliable as the electronic brain itself housed on the floor below his office with the silently-spinning wheels of magnetic tape and the clack-clack-clack of the punch cards. Indeed, it was his diligence and efficiency that had made his outburst cause for such concern in the department where he worked, as though fearing that a crack in the buttress would have the whole edifice crashing down if not tended to.

Farley Lustig had settled on his mother to feed to Doctor Solvang. His mother had not been the harridan that he described. She had been a pale, quiet woman. Mrs. Lustig had died when Farley was fourteen, sitting in her favorite chair, her chin on her chest, where she had fallen asleep watching television after washing up the dinner dishes. Within a few weeks Farley could not recall her face. Within six months he barely thought of her at all. As Farley's father had only recently been transferred to the army base in Tennessee where she chose to shuffle off this mortal coil, she had had no time to make friends with the other officers' wives, so only a handful turned up at her funeral to pay their respects.

Farley's father, Melvin Farley Lustig, on the other hand, had presided over his childhood like a titan. Big Mel had been at Anzio and Monte Casino at seventeen, having lied about his age to join up. He was a soldier's soldier, occasionally receiving phone calls from his old friend and former commanding officer General Omar Bradley. As the army was the only home and family he had ever known, he stayed on after the war and rose through the ranks. He had treated his only child like a raw recruit, making sure the boy knew all a boy should know about maintaining weaponry and getting a high shine on boots. It never occurred to Farley to hate his father. That would be immaterial. His father had never loved or been loved and would not know what to do with his son's affection. But Farley revered his father, the strength and power of the man, the way the soldiers under his father's command stiffened to attention when Big Mel came into the room, even though they might have their backs to the doorway through which Big Mel entered.

Growing up on army bases it had been obvious to Farley at a very early age that he was drawn to men. It was the young soldiers who populated his erotic imagination with their long legs and sinewy torsos and easy smiles. He was simultaneously aware that his father must never know this, and it was his father with his stoicism who showed the boy the way forward. Farley's face became a mask, betraying neither anger nor sadness nor delight. The military seemed the obvious course to take, hiding in olive drab anonymity. When Farley announced to his father that he had enlisted, his father said, "I wish you every success, son," and then assumed the stance that indicated to Farley that he was to throw a salute, which he did.

When he entered, the Korean Conflict was not drawing the attention of the United States Armed Forces, and Viet Nam had only started to swallow men and materials. Farley was attached to a supply company where his discipline and deference to his superiors ensured quickly that he rose to the rank of major.

But there was a flaw with Farley's plan. He hated the men who served under him. Their ease and camaraderie with one another, the intimacy that heterosexual men are capable of, unnerved and tormented him. Seeing one private clap another on the butt as they mustered would make his heart pound in his chest and earn them a bark to "Stop that fooling around!"

These details Farley did not share with Doctor Solvang. Neither did he mention Private First Class Emmett Johnson. Fat and fair-haired, Private Johnson was unremarkable. He kept to himself, drifting off to bury himself in some paperback book. But then came the day when Farley, walking across the base, behind his sunglasses, saw Private Johnson turn his attention from his book and let his gaze rest on Farley himself. Farley knew what that intent regard meant, knew just what was behind it. As Private Johnson passed out of his peripheral vision, Major Lustig could still feel the boy's stare filled with longing and desire.

Not three days later, Private Johnson was seven minutes late reporting for duty at his desk. At his own desk, Farley watched the advance of the second hand on his watch, listening for the sound of Johnson's typewriter, the indication that he had finally showed up. When he heard it he rose to his feet, turned, and walked through the desks of the other supply clerks who all fell motionless as he passed. In front of all of them, at the top of his voice, he berated Johnson, telling him he was a failure as a soldier, a failure as a supply clerk, and a failure as man. He did not relent when he saw the tears streaking the boys face. Neither did he relent when he saw the boy shaking. Nor when a wet spot sprouted and grew in the boys crotch.

After the dressing down, Major Farley Lustig ordered Private Johnson back to work. The young soldier sat in his soaked khakis, still shaking, still silently crying, until he was dismissed for lunch.

During lunch in the officers mess, Farley had heard the single gunshot, had paused to consider what the source might be, and continued eating his roast beef sandwich.

He was not bothered by the death by self-inflicted gunshot wound of Private Johnson, but his CO was. And so, without word or explanation, Major Lustig found himself transferred to a combat platoon in Viet Nam. Five weeks in, he and his convoy came under sniper fire and a bullet caught Major Lustig in the foot and another in his gut. When informed that he was going back to the States, he knew his military career was over. The G.I. Bill provided him with a free college education. He had been fascinated with the computers that had been slowly assuming more and more responsibility for supply operations at the Department of Defense, and decided to take courses in computer science. The demand was so great for even the most basic knowledge that he was recruited for a job after only five semesters.

"She lied to me," said Farley. "She told me that she had left the stove on. I had had toast and cold cereal for breakfast. I knew it was a lie, and I could see in her eyes that she knew I knew."

Doctor Solvang's pen jerked its way across the pad of notepaper in his lap.

Thinking back to college, Farley wanted to ask Doctor Solvang what he thought of the idea of Freud's that one of the professors in a required liberal arts class had explained with a smirk. Freud somewhere had said that distant ancestors of ours, before writing and possibly before language, had lived banded together in a tribe, an extended family, ruled over by a despotic patriarch, who they all feared and hated for his cruelty.

One day the sons could take their father's rule no longer. They rose up and tore him apart with their bare hands and then consumed his flesh. They were filled simultaneously with horror at what they had done and exhilaration at the freedom they experienced for the first time in their lives and terror at the implications of this freedom: would anarchy mean chaos and starvation? Each year, on the anniversary, they would recreate in ritual the murder of their father and god, although with some captured beast of prey. But with the iteration the bear or lion was replaced with a beast more easily managed from their domesticated herd, and then omitted altogether in favor of a feast. With every passing year the ritual became more mechanical and anemic; the original event was long forgotten.

Freud had explained culture—opera, literature, religion, the symphony, sport—as our attempt to revive the energy and power of that. Farley thought it explained much more. Farley thought that that story was the only true thing he had ever been told.

And what, he wondered, would Doctor Solvang make of the dark rituals that Farley himself had partaken in? He had been invited to a party. He would have to send a letter to a post office box and choose a name for himself that was not his actual name but which would go on the invitation list. He was not told the nature of the party in so many words, but was told that leather, black leather, if he owned any or could purchase any, would be appropriate attire. And he was assured that he would enjoy himself.

And he had enjoyed himself.

On the appointed night he had made his way to a nondescript industrial building in the West 30s. A freight elevator had taken him to the top floor, and there he entered a tastefully appointed apartment. Dinner was served at eight. He and fifteen other men were seated around a long, dark mahogany table. Conversation was boring, concerning the opera, the theater, and other subjects that held little interest for Farley Lustig. It could be any dull gathering of dull men were it not for the fact that they were waited on at table by footmen naked except for black leather collars buckled around their necks. The footmen retired after coffee, leaving the men to smoke their Cuban cigars that the host offered around. Then the host rose and announced, "Gentlemen, it is time."

The party followed the host, a fat man with a cherubic smiling face, across the wide entry hall to what Farley imagined on other nights was referred to as the "drawing room." Here crosses lined the walls, padded benches were positioned here and there, and mahogany library tables held a collection of belts, straps, flails, rope, and chain. The naked footmen knelt in formation on a plush Persian carpet. The men each chose one, and soon the spacious loft was filled with the sounds of punishment inflicted and cries and moans.

Farley had enjoyed himself very much.

The host had taken him aside at one point, offered him a brandy, and told him that he was "one of us" and would be invited back. The cherubic man, less cherubic with the executioner's hood he wore, asked what name he had given. "Hephaestus," Farley replied.

"Well, Hephaestus, I will leave you to your work and look forward to seeing you next month."

The crosses.

Farley, inventing more crimes of his mythical mother, looked at Doctor Solvang, who was relighting his pipe. With his stylish long blond hair, carefully trimmed beard, and deep blue eyes, Doctor Solvang looked like a pious Victorian painting of Christ.

The crosses.

Doctor Solvang, his wrists bound behind his back, wearing a flimsy white tunic, his head solemnly downcast; but perhaps the beard concealed a smug smile from his conversation with Pilate. The centurions prod and push Doctor Solvang along out to the porch where Farley is waiting, his eyes invisible in the shadow on his brow cast by his helmet.

Solvang raises his eyes and surveys Farley. Farley's face is impassive, as though he does not even see the son of a carpenter from Galilee at all. His mind only anticipates and relishes the task at hand. Farley gives a slight nod to his helmeted head, Solvang's hands are unbound, but before he has a chance to flex and stretch, he is pushed forward against a thick Doric column. The ropes are applied again, fastening the King of the Jews in an embrace of the marble cylinder. With a sword, the white tunic is removed, and Solvang stands naked. He shifts his weight from foot to foot, the muscles in his back tense and convulse. He is steeling himself. A tall centurion, a Carthaginian or maybe an Abyssinian by the looks of him, brings forward the cat-of-nine-tails and with a bow presents it to Farley, his captain. Farley lets the strands of thick leather run through his fingers and examines the iron nails attached to the ends. The Hebrew will bleed for him.

Farley positions himself at what he judges to be the correct distance, his right foot forward as though surprised mid-stride. Solvang lifts his bowed head, casting his eyes towards Heaven, praying, perhaps for strength. He will need all the strength he can summon, thinks Farley, and even that will not be enough.

Farley is still, not moving a muscle, his senses alive as they never are at any other time. He feels the heat of the midday Levantine sun, the faint perfume of a nearby stand of olive trees; somewhere a Hebrew boy, a shepherd, calls his sheep. Farley drinks it all in and inhales deeply.

Then he begins.

With a graceful motion, with his right hand, he sweeps the cat upwards from where it hangs suspended, the nails tapping the outside of his left calf when the wind stirs them. At the furthest extension, overhead and slightly behind him, he arrests his motion, and then in another sweep, focuses his attention on the knot of muscles between the Savior's shoulder blades, bringing the cat down. The leather braids slap the skin and the iron nails pass through the flesh as if it was water. Immediately Farley sees the streaks of the cuts, thin only for an instant and then thickening.

Solvang throws back his head and cries out, stifling the noise as soon as it escapes him as though embarrassed, as though he had stubbed his toe. His follow-through brings the cat back to where it began, and Farley raises it again for the next lashing, this time a little to the left. The leather and the iron catch some of the blood, already trickling from the first wounds inflicted, and inscribe a criss-cross pattern. "Two," says Farley aloud.

"You were how old? Eight? Nine?"

Farley Lustig considered the question. He stubbed out his cigaret in the large, circular ashtray on the coffee table between them.

"Eight," he replied.

"Did you cry? Surely most boys of eight, recognizing a mother's neglect for what it was, would have cried."

"I did not cry," answered Farley, "I don't remember crying."

"Did you think that crying would have been..." (Solvang, searching for a word, cast his eyes up and looked more than ever like Jesus.)

"Unmanly," Farley supplied. "Crying would have been unmanly."

New York City • October, 1985

From his second-floor apartment on West 80th Street, Farley Lustig watched the boy down on the sidewalk across the street from his apartment. Farley had heard somewhere that this is what Marlon Brando would do to James Dean, making the young actor wait outside the building where Brando lived, waiting for the signal to come in, waiting for hours. Farley was happy to recreate it with his own young actor.

He had no idea what Marlon Brando and James Dean got up to once they were together, but Farley credited himself with being more creative. On Ryan's last visit, a week prior, Farley had had the apartment in darkness except for the orange glow of the gas range in his small kitchen. As always, a door slightly ajar greeted Ryan when he climbed the stairs. The boy entered, closed and bolted the door behind him, took off his clothes, and got down on his knees.

This was their standard routine.

On that Friday night, however, Farley had sat for a while in the darkness, noticing Ryan notice the light from the burner blazing in the kitchen, seeing the look of confusion momentarily pass over the boy's face before it resolved itself into the usual calm expression.

That expression—jaw set, eyes downcast, a slight smile—was one of the things that Farley loved most about the boy, speaking as it did of his complete trust, obedience, and submission.

That Friday night Ryan had not even looked up as Farley came out of the darkness, stepped behind the boy, and applied first the leather hood and then the gag. Farley had clipped the leash onto the collar that Ryan now wore. The collar was custom made: braided latigo about the width of a thumb that ended in two loops. The two loops were secured with a padlock. Farley had the only key. In his daily life Ryan would wear the padlock in the back. But, Farley had noticed early on, when Ryan took up his post across the street, he would carefully move the padlock to the front.

With the hood and gag in place, Farley led the boy to the padded bench he had made. Once Ryan made contact, he knew the bench and knew to clamber up on it, relaxing as Farley buckled the thick black leather straps over the boy's forearms and calves, and across the small of his back.

Possibly, Ryan thought he was in for a fucking. In that he would be mistaken. Farley had another idea. He had begun with a paddling of the boy's butt, massaging and pinching his meaty glutes. Then he had repaired to the kitchen. Poised just over the flame was the work of a metalsmith in Jersey City, who made his living making wrought iron fences and staircases, but was happy to accept a commission for something slightly out of his line. At the end of a long, thin iron rod was a configuration of smaller flat pieces. These glowed a cheery deep red.

Taking the rod by the handle he had fashioned from soft leather straps wrapped around the opposite end, he carried it to the front room where Ryan was waiting.

"Boy, take a deep breath and hold it in," Farley ordered. He watched the young man's muscular back swell. He counted to himself, five . . . four . . . three . . . two . . . one, then decisively set the branding iron on the boy's right cheek. The gag did not entirely stifle Ryan's cry — that of a damned soul in Hell. The smell of a pork chop hitting the grill hit Farley's nose. He held the brand for just a few moments. When he released it, it adhered slightly to the boy's flesh. Ryan bucked and contorted, crying for all he was worth. Farley moved in to examine his handiwork. Just where the pocket of his jeans would sit, Ryan was now branded with an F L. It looked deep enough so that the brand would take. The boy would bear Farley's mark of ownership for the rest of his days.

Ryan kept up his sobbing as Farley removed the restraints. He removed the gag and instructed Ryan that if he made too much noise, back in it would go. Ryan nodded to show the order was received, understood, and would be obeyed.

He led the hooded boy over to the bed. He positioned himself and got comfortable, then took out his half hard dick and his balls. He snapped his fingers. Ryan moved forward until his knee collided with the leather covered mattress, then tentatively crossed the bed on his hands and knees. "Do something to take your mind off the pain, boy," Farley said. The boy's mouth found the dick of the man who owned him, whose brand he now bore, and set to work, tears still seeping from his closed eyes under the hood, now and then snorting snot.

Farley was eager to see how the brand had healed. He hoped that both letters would be distinct. He gave the signal, turning on the lamp that sat on the table near the window and pulling the curtains open. Ryan noticed immediately. He flicked his cigaret into a tree well and headed across the street in the early gloom of the November night.

Farley cracked open the door and waited.

Again Ryan entered, closed the door behind him, and stripped off his clothes, then sat down to put on his boots. Farley liked him naked except for his boots. As he got into position on his knees, Farley held up one hand. The boy stopped. Farley motioned him to rise and then to come forward, then to turn around. Ryan complied. Farley saw a grin on his boy's face. He allowed himself a smile.

The brand was perfect. Perfectly positioned, perfectly legible. Farley touched it tentatively. Ryan made a sharp intake of breath and recoiled slightly, then bent his head down further and relaxed. So it was still tender. Farley imagined Ryan going through his week. Would he have thought to cover the burn with antiseptic cream and a bandage? Would a bandage have made it more painful? Had he taken the next day off work to lie on his stomach in bed?

Ryan had standing orders. Every night at nine o'clock he called Farley. He would let the phone ring five times. If Farley did not answer, it was "as you were." If Farley answered (usually on the second ring), Ryan would receive further orders, such as, "Report at seven p.m. tomorrow." Ryan would reply, "Sir, yes Sir. Thank you, Sir!" and do as he was told.

Upon learning after the night that they had met at the Eagle that Ryan did not live in the City, Farley had told him to correct that. He had written the boy a check for five hundred dollars, told him to use it to open an account at a bank in the city, and if he needed more to tide him over until he found a place to live and a job, to let Farley know. ("And I want you to get a man's job," Farley had added, "I don't want a boy of mine being a waiter or a secretary.")

The five hundred dollars had been sufficient. On the bulletin board at his acting school, Farley found a notice posted that one of his fellow students was looking for a third to share an apartment with him and his girlfriend on the Lower East Side. The couple, with matching mohawks, had taken him on. Four months later, the girlfriend had decided to move to Los Angeles. As her father's co-signing had made the apartment possible in the first place, Ryan joined his housemate on the lease. Eight months later, the roommate had decided to move back to Northern Virginia, leaving Ryan alone in the alcove studio apartment on Stanton Street.

Ryan had at first found a job with a moving company. The irregular hours allowed him to go to auditions during the day. Then he found a job doing maintenance at a tech school serving the building trades. His shift was at night, again leaving his days free, and working at the school allowed him to take classes there at a discounted rate. The money from Farley had allowed him to repay his father for the cost of the vest and the boots. Only occasionally would the man he called Sir require him to report on a weeknight. When that happened, Ryan would call another member of the maintenance crew to fill in for him. All went smoothly.

When Farley had learned about the set up he was pleased.

Farley would rise early, pick up copies of the *Times* and the *Wall Street Journal* at a newsstand, and read them over while he ate breakfast at a neighborhood restaurant. Then he would take the subway to the tip of Manhattan and work the day away. After errands, a stop at the YMCA on 23rd Street, a simple dinner at home, and to bed. He wanted his days to be spent in a monotonous and mechanical routine. All his energies he kept in reserve like tinder, to be ignited when he ordered Ryan to report. Often they would pass the night with Ryan naked and chained at his boots, that subtle smile on his lips, while Farley read and smoked cigars. That was enough for both of them, and when Ryan kissed Farley's boots and offered gratitude for their time together, it was as sincere and heartfelt as when Farley allowed the boy to pleasure him or to beat the boy or fulfill whatever desires occurred to him.

As much as he could manage it, Farley wanted Ryan's life to mirror his. Not for a moment did he consider moving the boy in. He valued his privacy and his occasional nights out, but he did not want the clutter of the quotidian—washing up the dinner dishes, cleaning the bathroom, vacuuming the rug—to dilute the magic of the rituals and rites that Farley contrived when they were together. That, Farley believed, was what life was. Then, there was not time, there was only the two of them in an eternal moment, outside of time. Surely Ryan's life, lived alone in an unfamiliar city, had a similar shape.

Tonight, however, there would be something altogether different.

The parties in the loft that Farley had once attended had been supplanted by a club of sorts in the Meatpacking District. Every few weeks Farley would make his way to the Mineshaft. Mostly he would keep to himself, enjoying a Scotch whiskey that the bartender was amenable to stocking per his request. But, on occasion, he would feed a boy his piss or take off his belt and make a boy sing for him with grunts and lamentations. He wondered if the other men who frequented the Mineshaft noticed him and his reserve and if they wondered why. Tonight they would wonder no more. Word had passed that the club was closing its doors for good. Farley intended to take his boy there and show him off.

And so to work.

Ryan was restrained by the wrists to the length of chain that descended from an eye hook in one of the ceiling beams. He looked magnificent with his firm body, covered in blond fur, with the mop of blond hair on his head.

Farley whipped his shaving cream into a lather, and with a basin of hot water, proceeded to shave the boy clean with the steel safety razor he had inherited from his father. First the back, which was quick work. Then the armpits; and while shaving the chest he found that the blade began to tug, so he replaced it. Pulling up a chair, he made quick work of the boys legs. He paused now to rub witch hazel over the boy's now hairless skin, so smooth it was as though hair had never grown there at all. His eyes rested on Ryan's face, and his boy smiled at him. Farley's eyes raised slightly to the boy's thick head of curly hair, and the smile vanished. Seeing this, Farley suppressed his own smile.

First with a clippers, the boy was shorn of his locks, falling in wisps on the towel he stood on. Then, with another new blade, Farley turned his attention to the boy's scalp, shaving it clean, without nicking even once, watching the mix of emotions play on the boy's downturned face.

Now for the face. Farley lit a cigaret for himself and let Ryan have a few drags before he lathered up. "This barbering is something you should be doing for me," Farley observed. "Don't let it go to your head."

"No, Sir!" Ryan answered.

Farley had saved the best for last. He carefully shaved the boy's crotch and ass crack. Ryan's cock was hard, throbbing, and dripping precum with the novel sensation of Farley's touch there. Farley ignored this. The boy's gratification was not his concern.

After the boy endured the sting of more witch hazel, Farley stood back to admire his handiwork. This would fetch the top price on any auction block, he thought. But his eyes narrowed when he noticed Ryan's eyebrows. The only hair follicles left on the boy. They would have to go, too. And away they went.

Farley reached up and unbuckled the wrist restraints, but left them hanging from the ceiling. Ryan dropped his hands and rubbed them to chase the pins and needles.

"On the bed, on your back, boy," came the order.

Ryan obeyed.

Farley hauled a black duffle bag to the bed and as he did so, Ryan heard the tones of steel knocking against steel. Chains.

Farley opened the bag and pulled forth not just chains, but an ancient set of fetters and manacles, attached by chains to a thick steel collar. Farley had ventured far into *terra incognita* tracking these items down. He had admired some leg-irons, the prize possession of one of the men he had met at one of those dinner parties long ago. The man worked in Hollywood and had obtained them from a dealer in Madrid for a low-budget horror movie. Farley tracked the man down, obtained the name of the man in Spain, sent a considerable sum by money order, and waited weeks while his prize crossed the Atlantic. He did not know their provenance, although they looked old. He wondered if once he had his boy secured in them he would ever want to have them be empty again. In a photograph from an excavation in Italy he had seen the opened grave of a slave, and noted the thick iron collar where the skeleton's neck would have been. He liked the idea of his boy returning to dust before these bonds would. He applied the fetters first, happy that they fit snugly over the boy's boots. Then he fitted the manacles, like the fetters, closed securely with the turn of a special wrench that fit only these special bolts. Finally the collar.

"On your feet, boy."

As Ryan maneuvered himself off the bed, ancient chains clanked. There he was, like a seventeenth-century Irish seaman, captured by Moorish pirates, brought back to the Coast of Barbary in chains to begin his new, servile existence. The boy looked beautiful.

Farley went past the kitchen to the back room he had set up as his office. He dialed the phone and barked an order. He returned and lit a cigar and allowed his boy to enjoy a cigaret, standing swaying in his chains while they waited.

At the sound of a horn outside Farley drew on his heavy black leather jacket. With a padlock he secured a length of chain to a D-ring on the collar; this would serve as the tether for the night. Then, a black rubberized raincoat he had found at Goodwill was thrown over the boy's shoulders.. With his slave following behind him, fetters shortening his stride, his spine curved into a posture of submission by the length of the chain, the Master headed out into the night.

A long black car hummed at the curb. Farley had decided on a car service, as the drivers were well paid and if they noticed a man in leather with a man in chains bringing up the rear they would not make mention of it.

Bundled into the comfortable back seat of the Lincoln Town Car, Farley rolled down the window halfway and prepared to re-light his cigar.

"Smoking allowed?" he asked the driver.

"Absolutely, Sir. With the window lowered."

From his breast pocket Farley pulled his box of Marlboros and Zippo lighter and tossed them to Ryan. As the car made its way down the West Side, they smoked in silence.

Farley enjoyed cigars. He often smoked them when he was with his boy. He hoped that the smell of the smoke would become associated in the deepest parts of the boy's brain with him. Ryan sat smoking his cigaret, head down, examining his now smooth shaved body and the chains around his wrists and ankles. Farley noted that the cuffs fit the boy's wrists snugly without being tight, as though they had been made just for him. The special key was on the nightstand next to the bed. Ryan would wear those chains until Farley decided otherwise. A pride in ownership welled up in Farley. He extended an arm and let his hand rest at the back of his boy's collared neck.

Farley recalled his first time fucking a man. His name was Chuck. He was a Marine, nineteen years old, a few years younger than Farley was at the time. Both of them were in Bangkok for some "R and R." Farley saw Chuck look at him, then look away, then swallow hard, then look back. When Farley decided that the Marine was drunk enough on the bourbon he was putting away, he offered him a place to stay for the night. Once back at his hotel room Farley had decided that tying Chuck's hands behind his back would serve to disinhibit the Marine, taking over from where the alcohol left off. Chuck did not protest as the bootlaces were wound around his wrists and knotted. As Farley put him through his paces, calling the shots, he discovered what a joy it was having sex with another man. He had been completely a virgin before that night. Although he had never had sex with a woman, Farley imagined that women had to be treated with care. He had enjoyed forcing his dick down the Marine's throat and holding it there until he gagged and his face was red and tears filled his eyes. This only made his bound partner more zealous in his cocksucking. Men, Farley had concluded that night, don't mind when it hurts, when you're rough on them. They expected it, perhaps even enjoyed it more, like boys testing how tough they were in wrestling. "Rough and tumble play" he had heard it described.

Now the Lincoln Town Car crept through the meatpacking district. Steam rose from manhole covers, men in bloody aprons unloaded the skinned carcasses of cows and pigs and sheep from trucks, hauling them on their shoulders.

"Middle of the block," he called to the driver.

He spotted the solid white line on the otherwise unmarked door.

"Here."

Farley dug in his pocket for some bills and passed them up to the driver. Lowering his voice, he said, "Be back here in two hours. Wait if necessary."

"Yes, Sir!" the driver answered.

Farley and Ryan exited on opposite sides, the chains clinking. Farley pulled the raincoat higher over Ryan's shoulders. He took the end of the chain that dangled from the boy's collar. Ryan, hobbled by his fetters, followed behind Farley.

Through the door was a flight of stairs, wooden and bare. Farley mounted them halfway, and then stopped behind the line of men ahead of him.

At the top of the stairs, a gruff voice loudly said, "Not dressed like that you fuckin' ain't."

A brief imprecation, then the gruff voice simply and firmly said, "No."

Jostling on the landing, and the waiting men pressed themselves against the left wall to make room for a tall man wearing well-tailored evening formals. "I just thought you might appreciate a little va-ri-e-teee," said the man descending over his shoulder with a smile.

"You should know better, Phil," laughed the man on the landing above, "Plenty of time to go home and change."

The other men in line ahead of them, dressed in leather or denim, moved more quickly through the line. As they talked to the gruff man, one by one they moved off to the right, and the men on the stairs moved up one step. Then Farley mounted the last step on the landing. Farley presented a card and some cash. "Two," he said.

The man raised his eyebrows, smiled, and motioned for Farley to step to one side. He gave the once-over to Ryan, standing in his chains, the open raincoat showing him naked except for those chains and the boots he wore.

"You're supposed to have him in clothes until you get him inside," said the man.

"I could button up the raincoat," answered Farley with good humor. They were motioned off to the right, and the man turned his attention to the young man behind them on the stairs.

Led by the chain by Farley, Ryan followed into a bar room, shuffling through sawdust and crushed beer cans on the floor. A pool table stood in the middle of the room. No one was playing. Almost the only light in the room came from what looked like Christmas lights behind a large American flag that hung on the wall behind the bar.

The two made their way along the bar to the far end where sat a shirtless young man about Ryan's age at a folding card table. "Hi!" the young man greeted them, with an ebullience that didn't match the somber surroundings, "Clothes check?"

Farley swiped the old raincoat from Ryan's shoulders and handed it to the young man. Then he unbuckled and unzipped his way out of his heavy leather motor officer's coat. Beneath it he was dressed in a leather bar vest and tight leather chaps over Levis. The bulge in his Levis, offset by the tight chaps, earned him an appreciative look from the coat check clerk that Farley acknowledged with only a slight movement of his thick mustache that may or may not have indicated a smile.

Their business concluded, they turned from the coat check, passed the bar again, and came to a vestibule. Next to the vestibule, the door standing open, was a bathroom. On the floor of the bathroom knelt a naked man, so muscled that with a handlebar mustache and a barbell labeled "500 lbs" he could have been a pen and ink illustration of a sideshow strongman. As they paused passing the bathroom, the muscled man looked up at them, lowered his eyes, and opened his mouth. Through the vestibule they entered another room, as large as the bar room. The bar room had been empty except for a few pairs and trios of men in conversation. The backroom was considerably busier. Dead center of the room, hung from the rafters, were a pair of slings. In the sling closest to them was a very skinny, very hairy man with a close-cropped head and a round horseshoe coming out of his nostrils and two more shining metal horseshoes about the same size through each nipple. A burly man sat on a stool in front of the man in the sling, the finger of one glistening hand probing the supine man's asshole, while the other hand dipped into a can labeled "Crisco" that swayed from its own smaller chain. The two men were intent on each other. "Just breathe deep, just relax, just enjoy it, Mark. Just relax, open up, and let me in."

The man in the sling moaned softly, nodding his head as though entranced.

All of this was completely new to Ryan, other than in the pages of magazines. Ryan saw that there was another horseshoe of steel in the head of the penis of the man in the sling, one end coming out of the piss slit. Ryan was momentarily fascinated, his eyes going from nose to nipple to dick, in formation like the constellation of the Southern Cross. Ryan wondered what the pain was like having those steel semi-circles driven through flesh and cartilage.

There was a sharp crack like a gunshot. Farley and Ryan both looked further into the room. A middle aged man, looking like he could be a high school science teacher with his paunch and his horn-rimmed glasses, was restrained to a cross that leaned out from the wall at the bottom. Behind him stood a man with a whip, dressed vaguely like a cowboy with western boots, brown chaps, and a kerchief knotted around his neck. With a terse upward and downward motion of his wrist and forearm, another crack. The avuncular-looking man on the cross gave a slight yelp.

"Easy!" said the cowboy, "I haven't even started on you yet!"

In the center of the room, set off by vertical timbers, was a dark rectangular hole in the floor. Although he had seen it before, for the first time Farley realized the intention of the timbers was to create the effect of the opening of a mine. Hence: the Mineshaft. The rectangular hole was not a hole but an open trap door with a flight of stairs leading down. Farley in the lead, Ryan in chains following, they descended. Once below the level of the floor, all was darkness, but the sounds of men having sex, the guttural noises, the sucking, a "Fuck yeah Boss!!" filled the air. Here and there the end of a cigaret glowed. As they moved through the darkness towards the dim light of a hallway, they brushed leather and the naked skin of the men at the bottom of the mineshaft, felt hands exploring them, heard baritone voices beckoning them.

The hallway they entered was L-shaped. After the turn was a doorway opening to a room full of bathtubs. Bare bulbs illuminated the room, giving a warm glow. Farley and Ryan could see over the rim of the clawfoot antique tub nearest the door. In the tub, on his back, was a young man, clearly a teenager, wearing motorcycle leathers. Four men stood around the tub; two of the men thoughtfully stroked their cocks. The other two men, at either side of the tub, were shooting streams of piss from their own half-hard cocks, spraying the boy's face as his open mouth gulped as much as he could of their gifts. "You beautiful fucking piss pig!" said one of the men appreciatively. "Fucking look at him lap that up!"

"Thank you, Sir!" said the smiling boy in the bathtub.

At the end of the hallway was a doorway, opening into another bar room. As they entered Ryan recognized the song playing: "warm leatherette, warm leatherette, warm leatherette..." repeated a male voice. The bar itself wrapped around the room. There were about fifteen men in the bar, none of them were talking. Their eyes bored into the newcomers. Farley spotted an empty chair and moved towards it. He turned around to face Ryan. This was the first time he had looked at his boy since they entered from the street. Mostly he had been attuned to the reactions of the other men at the Mineshaft that night. And he was pleased by what he saw in their faces.

In his mind's eye he saw Ryan as he had appeared standing on the sidewalk on West 80th Street with his lank blond hair, flannel shirt, and jeans. Now the boy was transformed, not a hair on him, his fair skin the color of coffee with more milk than Farley liked. In the dim light Farley could just make out the freckles on Ryan's forearms and shoulders. The manacles and chain glinted. Farley felt his cock stiffen. "What did I ever do to deserve this?" he asked himself. He took a step closer to his boy. His hand reached around and gave a squeeze to Ryan's firm butt cheek. Then he lightly ran his fingertips over the boy's ass until he felt the brand.

"Mine," he thought.

As if reading his mind, Ryan grinned and gave a little laugh.

"Sir," he said, "thank you... thank you for bringing me here, Sir." He paused. Another grin. "Thank you so much, Sir."

Farley allowed himself a smile in return. He gave a firm slap to Ryan's butt, then stepped back. He snapped his fingers and pointed to the floor at the foot of the chair. Ryan settled himself on his knees in the bed of sawdust on the floor. He gave a slow, deep inhale. Farley liked the way that broadened his shoulders and swelled his chest. Farley brought his meaty hand to rest on the boy's head, admiring the smoothness. As if hair had never grown there. Ryan bowed his head and sat motionless.

Farley moved to the bar. The barman was a handsome redhead. Farley asked for two Budweiser's and slid a few dollars across the bar. He returned with the two beers to where Ryan waited for the man who owned him. Farley popped the top on one of the cans of beer and downed it in almost one swallow. The beer here in this bar, called the Den, was always good and cold. He saw Ryan's eyes move to the second can of beer, then to Farley, looking for a signal.

Farley bent back his head and emptied the last drops of the Bud into his mouth. Then he crushed the can and lightly threw it at Ryan, hitting the boy in the forehead. Ryan smiled, in on the joke, and lowered his head.

Farley cracked open the second beer, took a sip, and then drew the box of Marlboros and the lighter from the inside pocket of his leather vest. He lit a cigaret, inhaled deeply, and then passed it pinched between thumb and forefinger to his boy, who gave a heartfelt "Sir, thank you, Sir!" as he accepted it and began to smoke.

Farley lit another cigaret and then looked around the room as the two of them smoked.

A man leaning against the bar stood up and with heavy steps of his big boots approached Farley. He stood looking down at Ryan, whose eyes didn't move from Farley's boots.

"Don't suppose this slave is on the market, is he?"

Ryan's dick sprang to attention.

"He is not," answered Farley.

"Somehow I didn't think he would be," said the man.

"I'd pay good money to have him for a night," he continued.

"I bet you would," said Farley amiably, "but I have plans for him tonight."

"Well," said the stranger, "no harm in asking, I hope."

Farley tipped his beer at the man who then returned to his place along the bar.

Farley smoked and drank his beer.

"Boy," he said presently.

His boy turned his face upward, "Sir?"

"Take my dick out, boy."

Ryan's manacled hands went to work unbuttoning Farley's fly. Gently, he eased Farley's thick tool out of the zipper. And knowing at this point what was expected of him, gently released Farley's balls from the denim pouch.

"That boy in the tub isn't the only piss pig here tonight, is he, boy?"

"No, Sir!" said Ryan.

Although surprised the first time, Ryan had quickly taken to urinal service. The taste varied, depending, the boy supposed, on what Farley had eaten and drunk prior, but always there was an unmistakable taste. Ryan had tasted his own piss, and that taste was absent. An image crossed his mind of himself in a "blind taste test," like in the commercial for soda pop on television, correctly picking out the piss of the man who owned him and whose brand he wore from among other offered samples.

Farley felt the energy in the room change. He was sure that all of the men in the room snapped their eyes and inclined their heads when Ryan took Farley's dick in his mouth and waited. He didn't wait long. His mouth filled. He opened up his throat and let the warm piss flow down his throat and into his belly. With one hand Farley gave him a slight shove backwards, surprising the boy. The startled look on his face was sprayed with Farley's piss. When the stream subsided, Ryan licked his lips.

"Thank you, Sir!" he said, and Farley knew he meant it.

Farley lit another cigaret and passed it to the boy. Then he lit another for himself. He rose, went to the bar, and returned with two more beers.

"Damn good boy, you are," he said and this time handed a beer to Ryan.

Farley took the end of the chain tether and gave a tug. Ryan scooted closer. Farley's hand on the boy's head brought Ryan's head to rest as on a pillow on Farley's thigh. He wound one arm behind Farley's calf and sat happily at the boots of the man who owned him, enjoying his smoke and his beer.

In the Den were a few men in couples. For some of these men it was as though what they had seen shared between Farley and Ryan made them appreciate what they had in each other. They drew closer. Their hands explored one another. They kissed. Other men in the room looked at Farley and Ryan and felt longing, some of them envious of Farley, more of them envious of Ryan. Two of the men Farley knew from the parties in the loft entered with their own boy in tow. After getting their own beers they stopped at Farley's table. Their boy dropped to his knees between them. The three men conversed briefly while their boys, on the floor among the sawdust, cigaret butts, and beer cans, gave silent nods of acknowledgement to each other.

After a time the two men moved on. As the boy moved after them staying on his hands and knees, Ryan noticed that across his shoulders in lower-case Gothic script was tattooed the word "slave."

As he knelt there, one arm still embracing Farley's right boot, Ryan wondered if that was what he was, too. He associated the word with Africans brought to North America who worked in the cotton fields of plantations in the Deep South. In his eighth grade U.S. History textbook there had been an illustration, a woodcut of a slave auction, taken from an abolitionist pamphlet. The impression it had made on him was how cruel human beings could be towards one another. He also knew from church how the Children of Israel had been made slaves by the Egyptians and had been brought out of slavery led by Moses. Again, cruelty.

But now, sitting chained at the feet of a man whose orders he took delight in following, a man who sometimes beamed at him, a man whose expectations and the meeting thereof meant a great deal to Ryan, he wondered about slaves of the Greeks and slaves of the Romans. And the Turks. Didn't the Turks have slaves, too? Was it possible that cruelty didn't always define the relationship of slave and Master?

Also from church he remembered the story of the Roman Centurion who came to Jesus, concerned that the "slave whom he loved" was ill. Jesus offered to come heal the boy, and the Centurion stopped him, saying, Ryan thought, that it wouldn't be right: "I am not worthy that Thou shouldest come under my roof, but speak the word only and my slave shall be healed."

In the Bible story, Ryan remembered, Jesus commended the man and told him that when he got home he would find his slave, whom he loved, restored.

"His slave whom he loved."

Did this man love him? Somehow Ryan believed he did. Although he had never said so, Ryan, when he was with him, felt himself to be loved, and loved in a way that he had never been loved before, in a way that was very deep and true. I love him, the boy thought; that's for sure.

Ryan leaned closer to Farley, letting his body relax against the leather of the man's chaps.

He felt Farley's hand rest on the top of his head and stroke his now smooth scalp tenderly.

What could this be but love?

Farley's thoughts had been running along the same lines, although he reflected on how every moment he spent with the boy seemed to be outside of the flow of time where seconds succeeded each other and became minutes and minutes became hours. How long had they been sitting here? A half hour? Two hours? Farley decided not to look at his watch to get an answer.

Instead, he rose to his feet. Ryan sat back on his haunches. Farley started walking. Rather than standing upright, Ryan followed on his hands and knees as he had seen the other slave do. They followed their path in reverse, down the hallway, past the room in the tub (where, from what they could hear, the young piss pig was still happy in the bathtub), through the dark room, and up the stairs.

In the room at the top of the stairs the two men using the sling

had progressed. The seated man's arm was now buried past the elbow up the ass of the man lying in the sling. The two men stared at each other in wordless rapture, oblivious to the other men in the room. They had the Universe to themselves. Surely it would have broken their mood if they had seen Ryan's face. Until that moment the boy had not known that such an act was possible, let alone enjoyable, and he marveled at the man in the sling with the piercings. Master (if Ryan was a slave, that would make the man a Master) brought his chained slave, down on all fours, past the two men in the sling and came to stop at a second sling, this one without an occupant. Master snapped his fingers, Ryan tore his attention away from the fisting scene, and Farley pointed to the empty sling. Ryan's sphincter clenched. It was rare that Ryan felt afraid with Farley, but he felt afraid now. Not afraid that Farley would harm him—he had no fear of that ever, not even that first night they met—but rather he was afraid of disappointing the man. Ryan swallowed hard and rose to his feet. Slowly he turned around. As he set the weight of his butt in the stiff leather of the sling, his left leg began shaking, always the telltale sign. Slowly he leaned back, cantilevering his legs upwards.

Farley took hold of the boy's shackled feet, lifted them, and boosted Ryan all the way into the sling. There were clips on the chains suspending the sling, and Farley attached these to the D-rings on the cuffs that encircled the shafts of the boy's Redwing boots. He pivoted his torso slightly sideways and squeezed between Ryan's outstretched legs. Farley's hands moved down the now smooth skin of Ryan's muscular legs, then over his abdomen and chest. Finally, he roughly grabbed the boy's three-piece set, his cock and balls, and pushed them first to one side and then to the other. Ryan's crotch was completely shorn of his blond pubic hair. Farley gave a slight nod of satisfaction of his work earlier in the night.

Farley looked down at Ryan, Ryan looked up at Farley. Again they stood still as time flowed around them. With his left hand Farley took hold of his own cock and balls and flopped them onto Ryan's crotch. Farley was hard; Ryan, still unsure about what he was in for, was flaccid. Reading this in the boy's face, Farley's dick got harder.

Farley reached for a glob of Crisco. He rubbed it between his two hands to warm it up and liquify it and then started massaging it onto the shaft of his dick.

Ryan exhaled and sank deeper in the sling. He smiled, closed his eyes, and waited. He felt Master's fat dick slide past his as the man drew back, and then felt the head of it come to rest at his asshole. Inhale. Exhale.

Expecting a pushing, Ryan felt none. He opened his eyes. Master was looking at him, his face expressionless. With his hands he took hold of the chain and pulled sharply. The motion drew him slightly away from Farley. He released, and he swung slightly forward. The man's dick was waiting and the head slipped into Ryan's relaxed, welcoming hole. Ryan pulled again on the chain, again swung forward, and Master's dick moved deeper into him. Ryan quickly got the hang of this. By shifting his weight and tugging on the chain, soon he was riding that dick, with the girth and heft he had come to love. Farley started to help, not by moving his hips, but by pushing on Ryan's thighs. Gently Ryan swung to and fro in the sling. The motion gave him a feeling of weightlessness. Master's dick became his connection to the earth as he floated in the air. Now, with his sphincter open and relaxed, the man's dick was going all the way out and all the way in, alternately filling Ryan and then leaving a momentary void inside him. All fear, all anxiety gone, Ryan felt only pleasure, warm and wonderful pleasure. How could he have not recognized what Master felt for him as love before tonight? Master had chosen him, Master had made him his own, Master had led and he had followed, and where they went together was wonderful.

"Uhhh... uhhh... uhhh..." Ryan vocalized. He looked up at the man fucking him and that man's slave let out a bellow of joy. Farley let out a bellow of his own and felt himself explode inside the boy. Ryan felt this explosion, too, felt Master's member pumping his load into him. Now the boy babbled, again laughing and crying at the same time, the love he felt pouring out of him in a torrent. The man's dick still inside of him, still throbbing, he strained to right himself in the sling. Farley let go of the chains suspending the sling, reached forward and wrapped his arms around Ryan, drawing his slave close to him in a tight embrace, rocking him gently, tickling his neck with his mustache. He felt tears spring from his own eyes: this boy... this handsome young man ... belonged to him. Was owned by him: body, spirit, and soul. His to cherish, his to fuck, his to mark with his brand, with the red imprint of his hand and his belt; his slave, taking his love, taking his piss, taking his violence.

As Farley held him, he seemed to grow in size. He was a giant. Ryan was being held by a giant of a man — a man so strong, so powerful, who loved him so much that in his arms, by his side, no harm could come to him. He was safe, as safe as any man could ever be. He was this man's slave.

They held each other, drawing sighs, now and then a shudder from one or the other. Ryan's manacled hands were clasped under his chin, Farley's strong arms enfolding him still, gently stroking his slave's back, neck, and scalp.

Their heart rates slowed to a normal rhythm, Farley relaxed his hold, and Ryan eased backwards into the sling. As their bodies came apart they both became aware that Ryan had shot his load too, spurting all over his belly and chest, and like glue it had cemented them together while they embraced.

Farley unhooked the clips and gently lowered his slave's legs until his booted feet were again in contact with the floor and Ryan was upright again.

Farley took hold of the chain that served as the leash for his slave, gave a sharp tug, and turned. Ryan, head bowed, followed him. They stopped at the coat check. As the smiling man handed them Farley's coat and the rain coat, he said he hoped they had a good night.

As they descended the stairs out into the night, Ryan's eyes again focused on the lights, the man still posted at the top of the stairs, the back of Master's head with its dark, close-cropped hair.

On a white piece of paper stapled to the wall of the stairwell, Ryan was surprised to see a drawing of a bald-headed hairless man on his knees, looking up at a leather-wearing man looming over him. Printing above the image read, "So you want to be a slave... This Wednesday, 7 PM, at the Lesbian and Gay Community Center, 208 West 13th Street, GMSMA will present a panel discussion of real slaves who will tell you what it's like."

New York City • May, 1989

"We've been at this for an hour. We have some cookies and beverages, soda and coffee, so I suggest we take a break," said Tom Tomlinson, expert bondage top, flown in from San Francisco for the occasion. "Except for you, boy!" he added, which got a laugh from the eighteen men assembled for the suspension bondage dungeon demo.

Ryan hung in the air, like a still photograph of a man on a trampoline.

As the crowd made their way to the folding table where the snacks had been set out and where the coffee urn had finally ceased gurgling, indicating that the coffee was brewed, Chip broke away from the group and came to survey his mid-air friend. "I'll take care of you, Sweeney. What's your poison? Sugar cookies? Peanut butter? And how do you take your coffee again?"

"I'm fine," said Ryan, with as much of a shrug of his shoulders as the ropes would allow him.

"Are you sure? I got you into this predicament."

"Predicament bondage was two months ago," said Ryan, "and I know, because I was the demo bottom for that, too."

Chip and Ryan had both showed up for the first time at the same GMSMA meeting, and they were nearby one another when the President of the organization asked if anyone was interested in membership. They had known each other by sight. Ryan, with the many skills he had learned at the Manhattan Vocational Technical College, and finding that being a good actor in Bucks County, Pennsylvania, had not translated to being a good actor in New York City, had found a job he liked and which paid his bills working for a company that made props for the theater. Chip was the assistant to a much sought-after set designer with two Tony awards to his credit.

Both of them had signed the membership application bending over a card table, sharing the same pen, and pieced together why each was familiar to the other.

"Nice collar," Chip had said, eyeing the intricately braided leather closed with a padlock around Ryan's neck. "Who's the lucky Dom?"

After explaining to Ryan that "Dom" was a catchall term for Master, Daddy, Sir, and other permutations, Ryan confirmed that he was indeed a slave. It felt like an intimate confession. He had never told anyone else about his trips up to West 80th Street and his vigils on the sidewalk.

Chip told Ryan that he had been collared until recently, but it hadn't worked out.

Nothing in Ryan's experiences with the man who owned him gave him any idea what "not working out" entailed.

After the GMSMA program meeting, devoted to "100 ways to tie a man to a bed," they had gone together to Florent, a few blocks away from the Center in the meatpacking district, and enjoyed excellently prepared American Diner Haute Cuisine that the restaurant offered. Ryan had asked Chip what "not working out" meant, and the explanation (Chip's Daddy had tried to move too fast, getting into things that Chip didn't feel he was ready for) left Ryan even more confused.

Ryan gave a brief account of meeting the man whose collar he wore all those years ago at the Eagle. Again, no one but Ryan and Farley Lustig knew this story. Ryan mentioned, almost in passing, that he had been branded.

"Wow! That's hard core!" responded Chip, "did you need a lot of preparation for that?"

"Not too much," replied Ryan. "He put a hood on me and and tied me down to a bench."

"No," Chip clarified. "I mean, when he told you he wanted to brand you—and it's a real brand we're talking about, right?" Ryan explained that the branding iron that was used now hung above the sealed fireplace in Farley's office at home. "What did you say? How did you negotiate that?"

"I'm his slave," Ryan offered. "He just did it."

The server brought their food. They dug in in to the excellent fare and conversation was momentarily interrupted.

"So where do you guys go together? My Daddy once took me on a run with Excelsior, the motorcycle club. Do you go to the Eagle?"

After a few more questions and answers, Ryan and Chip realized that they were talking at cross purposes. That night Chip had dubbed Farley "Mister Benson," after the character in the fictionalized accounts of Mastery and slavery by John Preston. Or "Mister B." for short.

Together they had joined GMSMA, and together they had decided to serve on the Membership Committee, the principal duties of which were to provide snacks at the Wednesday night GMSMA program meetings.

After being shaved before the trip to the Mineshaft, Ryan kept his blond hair close cropped and continued to shave his crotch and the crack of his ass. Chip's hair was dark brown and fell to his shoulders. They were the same height and roughly the same build, and as they were always seen together, the other members of GMSMA thought of them as a unit of sorts. And both of them were constantly called upon to take the sub role in dungeon demos and educational programs. "boys… would either of you be available the second weekend in November…?" was the way the question was posed.

When Master Chaz, a soft-spoken and fussy man who organized the dungeon demos had asked both of them which one would like to be the "demo bottom" for suspension bondage, Chip, who was slightly claustrophobic, had volunteered Ryan. Thus, the padded bondage table on sawhorses having been removed, the configuration of ropes that Tom Tomlinson referred to as "Brooklyn Bridge" held Ryan aloft.

Chip moved off to talk to the other men attending the demo, leaving Ryan alone with his thoughts.

GMSMA, Gay Male S/M Activists, had been eye-opening for Ryan. Other than the people he worked with, he had known no one in New York City other than Farley. He was either at work, at one of the few inexpensive restaurants where he ate alone, criss-crossing Lower Manhattan auditioning for parts in small off-off-off-Broadway theater companies, at home alone in his alcove studio apartment, or, it seemed, at the feet of his Master in Farley's apartment on the Upper West Side. Being collared, naked except for his boots, giving boot service, taking a beating, occasionally spending the night, feeling Farley's hands on his body, obeying the commands he was given: this constituted what Ryan thought of as "his life"; the other parts were little more than filling time between those trips to West 80th Street.

GMSMA had changed all of that. For members, educational workshops, the Wednesday night programs, meetings of special interest groups, happened every weekend and some week nights from September to June. Ryan went from knowing no one to knowing dozens of men, a collection of Dominants and submissives and switches, elected and appointed officers in the organization, recognized experts in the theory and practice of BDSM: Bondage, Domination, Sado-Masochism.

As Farley almost never asked questions of his slave, and Ryan never spoke other than to respond to a command, this venture had gone undiscussed with one exception.

One night at Farley's, handcuffed and on his knees, the Master had presented his slave with a copy of *Newslink*, a publication produced by GMSMA. On the cover was a photograph of him and Chip, arm in arm, with rows of clothespins running from their knees to their collar bones.

"This is you, isn't it, boy?" Farley had asked.

"Sir, yes, Sir," Ryan had answered. "It was at an educational event, teaching about BDSM, Sir."

"Education," Farley had said, not as a question, just as a statement. He thumbed through the pages of the booklet.

"When you try to put lightning in a bottle, do you know what you end up with, boy? You end up with a bunch of empty bottles, each labeled 'lightning.'"

That was the only discussion they had ever had about Ryan's affiliation with GMSMA.

GMSMA had also introduced Ryan to the watchwords, "Safe, Sane, and Consensual" BDSM. Chip was a big proponent of this idea. When Chip would question whether or not what Ryan and his owner got up to fit these criteria, Ryan would explain that with his Master he never felt safer. His slavery was safety itself.

But like a faint odor brought in on the breeze, Ryan began to doubt his status as slave.

A big part of "safe" was refraining from the exchange of bodily fluids. Condoms were encouraged, and one of the great things about BDSM in the minds of many members of GMSMA was that a good time could be had by all without any bodily fluids coming into the picture at all, as, for example, was the case with suspension bondage. When his Master fucked him, on those wonderful, glorious occasions, no condoms were involved. His Master's "bodily fluids" were deposited deep inside Ryan.

Ryan never revealed to Chip or to anyone else that the sex that he was having would be deemed "unsafe."

During his time as a member of GMSMA, Ryan had come to know men who died. Often it had been terrible to watch. Handsome, smiling men started to appear gaunt and frail when they attended meetings; then they stopped attending meetings. Then there was an announcement about what hospital they were in if you wished to send a card or flowers, and then an announcement of a "celebration of life" or services in some church.

All of this, from what Ryan understood, was the result of the exchange of bodily fluids at some point.

Ryan's father and mother had been high school sweethearts, marrying when they were eighteen and nineteen. All four of Ryan's grandparents were still living. He had never known death close at hand. Death was something that happened to one of the old men or women at the church his family had attended, their names mentioned in the bulletin under a line drawing of three crosses against a rising sun. But now, death seemed to be walking the same streets as he was, in the same room, pausing to tap men close at hand on the shoulder.

"Get tested!" urged GMHC at a booth outside of the Gay and Lesbian Center on West 13th Street as Chip and Ryan walked to a meeting of the membership committee. Both of them took handfuls of condoms offered with a joke: "Are you sure this is going to be enough for you guys?"

"I don't need to, but you should," said Chip. "You're doing that, right?"

"Do what?" asked Ryan.

"Get tested," said Chip.

Ryan's thoughts pulled up short. Something Chip had just said...

"Why don't you need to get tested?" he asked.

"Let's smoke before we go into the meeting," Chip said.

The two young men lit their cigarets and slowed their pace, heading towards Eighth Avenue.

"I'm HIV positive," said Chip. "I found out a year and a half ago."

Ryan stared.

"It's okay," Chip continued, "I've got plenty of T cells."

As often happened, Ryan had no idea what Chip was talking about but pretended that he did. "Words, words, a little air between the lips," he thought to himself. He and Chip had gone to see Shakespeare in the Park the previous Summer. When the actor spoke that line, Ryan had looked at his friend beside him.

"So I'm healthy. I eat well. No more seafood. No more red meat. And I've started doing acupuncture. I could live to be an old failed actor," he smiled, "still looking for a Daddy."

When the suspension bondage dungeon demo was over, Ryan was released from the ropes. Tom Tomlinson, the expert bondage top from San Francisco, gave him a warm hug, telling him it was a pleasure. Ryan helped Chip box up the unused cookies, the packets of sugar, and the powdered creamer. He unplugged the coffee urn and headed down the hallway to pour the leftover coffee down the toilet.

When he returned from the errand, he found Chip sitting on a chair, massaging his temples.

"Ryan," he said in a weak voice, "could you take care of this stuff? Take it down to the storage area in the basement? I've got this headache."

Ryan did as told. When he returned, Chip was pale, sitting with his head between his knees.

"Chip..."

"Ryan, fuck, it hurts so bad. I think I need to go to St. Vincent's."

St. Vincent's Hospital was half a block away on the corner of 13th Street and Seventh Avenue. His arm around Chip's shoulder, Ryan steered his friend out of the building and down the sidewalk.

The emergency room was chaos. It looked to Ryan as though half of the people waiting to be treated were gaunt, skeletal men, their hands shaking as they sipped water out of paper cups. As they waited, Chip closed his eyes tightly and leaned against Ryan. "What the fuck, what the fuck, what the fuck," repeated Chip.

"Just hold on." I think they're almost ready for us," said Ryan.

That was not the case.

Three hours later they still sat in the same vinyl upholstered chairs, and, it seemed to Ryan, none of the people who were seated around them had risen when a name was called by a nurse wearing surgical gown, gloves, and a face mask.

Chip's whimpering had subsided. He leaned against Ryan, resting his head on Ryan's shoulder. Ryan wondered if he had fallen asleep. Not wanting to wake him, Ryan slowly and carefully leaned forward, then twisted his head to look at Chip's face.

Chip was not asleep.

Chip's eyes were wide open. His mouth gaped. A thin strand of drool descended from his mouth. "Chip..." said an alarmed Ryan.

At the mention of his name Chip's body spasmed, his head turned with a jerk, his unseeing eyes passing over Ryan. Chip lurched forward, tumbling out of his chair and onto the linoleum floor. Face pressed into the floor, his butt in the air, Chip's muscles twitched and contracted. "Geh geh geh geh..." Chip intoned, keeping time with his spasms.

"Nurse! Help! HELP!!" screamed Ryan.

Two figures in scrubs appeared, their faces hidden by the surgical masks. "Seizure," said the female one to the male one.

"Help him! Please!" pleaded Ryan on the floor now, trying to stop Chip's head from pounding the floor.

The two greenish-blue figures didn't move.

"Please! Help him! Make it stop!"

"AIDS?" asked the male.

"What?" cried Ryan.

"Does this man have AIDS?" asked the male.

"He had a headache," answered Ryan, weeping, "I brought him here because he had a headache. Please do something..."

A gurney arrived. More figures in scrubs hoisted Chip's seizing form, like a puppet, up onto the gurney, an injection was administered, and almost at once the spasms became less pronounced. Chip continued to make the "geh geh geh geh" noise, still with his unseeing eyes popping from his head, scanning the room.

Ryan was trembling as the gurney carrying Chip was propelled away. The male figure stayed behind. "Your 'friend,'" he asked Ryan, "does he have AIDS? Is he HIV positive?"

"He's positive. He has HIV," Ryan answered, "but he told me it was fine. He said he was healthy. He had a headache."

The male figure, without saying another word, followed the gurney.

Ryan slumped in his seat. Another figure in blue-green scrubs and a surgical mask and gloves appeared with a spritz bottle and a roll of paper towels and went to work on the puddle of saliva tinged pink with Chip's blood on the linoleum floor. The smell of bleach filled Ryan's nostrils.

"Charles Hayes," said Ryan for the third time that night. "They took him away around midnight."

"I'm not showing any information yet, Sir," said the woman, peering at her computer screen.

His seat had been taken—all the seats had been taken—so Ryan stepped outside to smoke. After only a few drags, he thought better of being outside when the automatic door gave the sound of someone in a white lab coat and the inevitable face mask calling out, "Mr. Boatwright?? Mr. Boatwright?" No seats being available, Ryan found some available wall space and sat on the floor. Whenever he would begin to drift off to sleep, he would see Chip's terrible face. The sky had gone from black to pale outside when Ryan, half asleep, heard, "Anyone here with Charles Hayes?"

Crawling the first ten feet, mentally and physically spent from the ordeal, he staggered towards the voice.

"I'm sorry to tell you that Charles died at one o'clock this morning." The doctor, who seemed to be about the same age as Ryan, paused only a moment as Ryan began to cry, and continued: "We believe he had a sinus infection. As his immune system was impaired from the HIV, his body was unable to fight it. The infection backed up through the sinuses into his brain. Very likely he had no idea what was happening to him."

Ryan was now blubbering.

"Are you a blood relation? Do you have any information about who his next of kin might be?"

Ryan had nothing to offer. He knew that Chip was from St. Louis.

For the gay men who gathered at the Fifteenth Street Quaker Meetinghouse for the celebration of life for Charles "Chip" Hayes, the experience had dulled into routine. Attendance was sparse. The first to speak was a man named Thales Bryce, Chip's boss, whose donation to the Society of Friends had secured the space for two hours—and only two hours, as another celebration of life was coming in immediately afterwards. Thales Bryce spoke solemnly about Chip's energy and spirit, his willingness to stay late, working around the clock when need be, to get the job done. He would have a hard time finding someone to replace him.

Having given vent to his frustrations at getting good help these days, Bryce returned to his seat, near Ryan. The next speaker was a stocky man named Joe, who was chair of the membership committee of GMSMA. Thales Bryce was seated so close to Ryan that Ryan saw his eyes follow the man as he crossed the room and heard him give a snort of disapproval. Ryan wondered why. Joe was wearing a tight black t-shirt, jeans, boots, and a leather vest with GMSMA's club patch on the back.

Joe was a magnetic speaker, with a gift for holding the attention of his audience. He, too, spoke of Chip's reliability, but also mentioned his friendliness and sexiness. Ryan saw Thales Bryce entwine his white-knuckled fingers and grow red in the face as though on the verge of an outburst. Again Ryan wondered what could be the cause of his consternation. Joe then spoke of how we should not get used to burying young men. "As someone who is himself living with HIV," he said.

Ryan felt tears well in his eyes. He pulled himself together. Joe had asked him before they got started if he would say a few words.

Ryan felt very lonely. Lonely and afraid. He had not realized until that day how much Chip and the companionship that Chip offered to him had meant. New York City suddenly seemed an empty, haunted place. He felt himself adrift, like a leaf blown on the wind. He remembered the suspension bondage demo, when Chip and everyone else tended to snacks, and he was left alone, hanging in midair, without purpose, without comfort.

An image of his Master arose in his mind, but then just as

quickly vanished. Since that night at St. Vincent's Ryan had not made his nightly phone calls to the man. The man never called him. He always called the man. As the years had rolled by a measure of flexibility was offered him. He need no longer call at nine o'clock sharp. Also, the man had gotten an answering machine. On the nights that Ryan would call, when the man didn't pick up, he would hear the gruff, gravely baritone: "I am not here to take your call just now. Leave your message."

Ryan's fingers felt the padlock suspended from the braided black leather underneath the ill-fitting white button-down shirt and tie he had bought at The Gap for the occasion. He noticed that he was the only person there wearing a necktie, but it was the first celebration of life he had attended.

Joe wound down his remarks. There was a smattering of applause as he returned to his seat. This seemed out of place to Ryan.

Ryan did not trust himself to use his own words. His actor's instinct told him to select the words of another, commit them to memory, and have those come out of his mouth. He had remembered a movie from a few years previously, *Out of Africa*. In the movie Meryl Streep's character had recited a poem. Ryan remembered the sentiment of the poem and was able to track it down with the help of the librarian at the front desk of the New York Public Library's main branch.

Ryan rose, walked to the middle of the room, which he thought of as "center stage," took note that, as there were people sitting on all four sides, he would have to address his audience theater-in-the-round style. He paused, as though collecting his thoughts; then he began:

> The time you won your town the race
> We chaired you through the market-place;

Man and boy stood cheering by,
And home we brought you shoulder-high.

Today, the road all runners come,
Shoulder-high we bring you home,
And set you at your threshold down,
Townsman of a stiller town.

Smart lad, to slip betimes away
From fields where glory does not stay,
And early though the laurel grows
It withers quicker than the rose.

Eyes the shady night has shut
Cannot see the record cut,
And silence sounds no worse than cheers
After earth has stopped the ears.

Now you will not swell the rout
Of lads that wore their honors out,
Runners whom renown outran
And the name died before the man.

So set, before its echoes fade,
The fleet foot on the sill of shade,
And hold to the low lintel up
The still-defended challenge cup.

And round that early-laureled head
Will flock to gaze the strengthless dead,
And find unwithered on its curls
The garland briefer than a girl's.

Those assembled filed out of the meetinghouse. Chip's sister, the only member of his family to make the trip, stood outside the door. She had been Chip's younger sister. She was a senior in college. Her face red but composed, she accepted the

condolences of strangers.

Ryan wondered where Chip's parents were. He wondered, though, if his parents would make the drive to Manhattan from Chalfont, Pennsylvania, to sit among strangers and hear stories of a man who would be unrecognizable to them.

Outside Ryan loosened the tie, then removed it, crumpled it, and put it into the pocket of his pleated gray cotton pants. He lit a cigaret and looked out at the park across the street, dotted with encampments of homeless people. New York City constantly served up contrasts and contradictions, even to the visitor whose time there was as brief as a few hours on a late afternoon.

"That was wonderful what you said," said a voice behind him.

Ryan turned. He looked into the eyes of Thales Bryce.

"You were Chip's friend, weren't you?"

Ryan nodded.

"He must have meant a lot to you." Thales smiled warmly. "At least you have decided to dress appropriately for the occasion."

Ryan understood Thales' earlier upset. It was the leather worn by the members of GMSMA in attendance.

"Chip was a very good friend," Ryan said.

"I was his employer. He worked for me," Thales clarified unnecessarily. "My name is Thales. Thales Bryce. It's an odd name, I know. I grew up in Nashville. In parts of the South there is a tradition of giving family names that die out as first names. My mother's mother was Nomia Thales."

"Huh," answered Ryan, "It's a nice name. I like it."

"And I," said Thales, "would like to have dinner with you sometime. I really didn't know Chip outside of work and I feel as though I missed out. I would enjoy hearing you tell me about him."

He handed Ryan a card on thick stock with his name, street address, and a phone number.

Hands in his pocket, Ryan walked back to his studio apartment on the Lower East Side. The sun was setting as he arrived home and climbed the four flights of stairs. The hallways smelled of cooking, although none of the smells was familiar to him.

In his apartment he sat down on his bed. As he withdrew his hand from his pocket, Thales' card came out with it. He read through the fine script.

What to do, what to do. He thought of Thales. He thought of Chip. Through the iron security gate on his rear windows, through the green leaves of the ailanthus trees that grew in the small square of soil behind the tenement building where he lived, the sky had turned a deep indigo.

Ryan lay back on his futon mattress and was asleep almost as soon as his head hit the soft mattress.

He awoke in darkness. A thought occurred to him — it was Sunday night. A few times Chip had dragged him to a club night on the West Side Highway. Ryan had the impression that the other nights of the week the club was straight, but on Sunday nights, a promoter named Chip held an event called "Mars Needs Men." ("We Chips have to stick together," Chip had said the first time he talked Ryan into going with him.)

Ryan thought that a dark room, booming music, and the contorting bodies of men would help him. He could imagine Chip there among the dancers, momentarily separated from him.

Ryan changed clothes. Black jeans, a black t-shirt, and his Redwing boots. He tumbled down the stairs, walked a block, and found a cab.

Outside the club was posted a doorman encircled by velvet ropes.

Chip had instructed him on how this particular game was played. Ryan stood at the rope, did not make eye contact with the doorman, and gave his face a faraway look as though he was thinking of something else, something involving sex. Two younger men next to him were doing everything wrong. They beamed anxiously at the doorman who in turn ignored them. After opening up the ropes to a group who warmly greeted the doorman by name, he closed them again and then came over to Ryan.

"How many?" he asked.

"Just me," Ryan answered.

The rope was opened. "Enjoy your night," said the doorman, returning to his conceit of being oblivious to all the people standing at the ropes.

Ryan dug money out of his jeans and paid the entrance fee. The ground floor was a riot of flashing lights and music. The dance floor was packed. Ryan spotted the stairs and climbed to the next floor. This room had a bar and a happenstance arrangement of thrift-shop sofas. Ryan got himself a bottle of Rolling Rock and continued his climb. On the uppermost floor the lights were not so insistent. The DJ, working his turntables from a platform only about eight inches above grade, was more a part of the crowd than removed from it. This floor was not so crowded.

Ryan downed what was left of his beer and discarded the bottle. Bopping slightly, he made his way to the middle of the dance floor. He closed his eyes, feeling the throb of the bass in the bones of his chest. "Back to life, back to reality..." sang a melodic voice over a minimal beat. "However do you want me, however do you need me?"

Ryan let his body move to the music, keeping his eyes closed. Chip was there, a better dancer than Ryan was, droplets of his sweat catching Ryan in the face when he threw his head back. Ryan smiled. It was alright. Everything would be alright. His mind went blank; he only heard the music, and that crowded out his thoughts, his sadness, and his anxieties. He let the DJ sweep him away, taking him on a journey with the tracks the man played.

Ryan, oblivious to his surroundings, was brought back to his body by the sensation of a hand brushing his right nipple. He opened his eyes. Right in front of him was a well-built man, also in a black t-shirt and black jeans. The man also wore a black wool watch cap that framed his broad face. His face was unshaven, the shadow of the stubble giving contour at the cheekbones and the cleft of his chin. Thicker than the stubble were the sideburns the man wore. The man was smiling at Ryan.

Ryan closed his eyes again. Slowly, slowly, he moved forward. He began to feel his arms and hands brush against the other man. The other man's hand landed on Ryan's hip and sat there, holding it gently as Ryan swayed to the music. Ryan's opposite hand extended until he felt the man's chest. Softly, Ryan's hand moved around the man's flank, not losing contact, and came to rest in the small of the man's back. Now their torsos bumped each other. Both men moved closer still. Both of the man's hands were now on Ryan's hips. Ryan moved his other hand around to join at the small of the man's back. Their motions slowed, they lost time with the music. Ryan felt the scratch of the man's razor stubble on his upper lip. He opened his mouth and received the man's tongue. Now their bodies ceased to sway; they held each other, kissing deeply, eyes closed. The only sensation was the warm touch and embrace of another man; the sound of the music seemed distant.

The man's mouth gently pulled away from Ryan's mouth. Ryan felt the scruff on his left ear.

"Wanna get out of here?" the man asked.

They joined hands, and Ryan was led down the stairs. He admired the man's wide, thick back and muscular arms. His muscularity made him seem so virile, so alive. Out on the sidewalk both of them lit cigarets. They exchanged names. The man had a foreign name, possibly German or Israeli. Ryan didn't quite catch it. Before Ryan could ask him to repeat it, they kissed again. This time their kiss was smoky.

"I live right up in Chelsea," said the man." We could go there."

"Sure," said Ryan.

Cabs were idling in a line at the curb outside the club. They climbed into the back of the cab at the front of the line. The man gave the driver the address, and they were off. As the cab sped north on the West Side Highway, they smiled at each other. The man squeezed Ryan's thigh and winked.

In minutes the cab pulled up. Ryan dug in his pocket, but the man said, "Naw, I got it," gave the driver some bills and told him to have a good night. His was a modern building. They entered through a glass door and rode up in an elevator, kissing again. In the man's third floor apartment the door closed behind them, the man hauled off Ryan's black t-shirt and then his own, smiling at Ryan and then fumbling with Ryan's belt and the buttons on his fly. Ryan took over.

"Want a beer? Water? I think I have apple juice..." the man offered.

"I'm good," said Ryan.

As Ryan unbuttoned his jeans, he realized his boots would have to come off first. He sat down on an ancient club chair — the only furniture in that room other than a café table with two chairs covered with unopened mail. He hauled off his boots, shucked his pants, grabbed his t-shirt from the floor, and made a pile of his clothes.

The man had kept pace with him. Ryan was now only in white boxer shorts, the man in white briefs. They kissed again, their hands exploring each other's bodies. The man was hairy. Ryan ran his fingers over the man's chest. The man's hands ran over Ryan's ass. As the man guided him though the only door to the small bedroom, the man's forefinger tickled the stubble on Ryan's shaved ass crack and dug between the two mounds of muscle and swirled on Ryan's asshole. Ryan moaned.

"Like that?" asked the man with the foreign-sounding name.

"Yeah," said Ryan.

"Good," said the man.

The man pushed Ryan backwards onto an unmade bed and followed him. The man kissed Ryan again, but then quickly withdrew, then giving Ryan a kiss on the chin. Then Ryan felt the stubble of the man's lips on his throat. The man dragged his chin down Ryan's chest, giving little kisses and bites along the way. His mouth found Ryan's left nipple. He sucked, then gently applied his teeth, then flicked his tongue at the tip of the nipple. Ryan sighed and let his hands fall back on the bed

above his head.

"Good boy," said the man, startling him slightly to be addressed like that. At either side of his licking, kissing mouth, the man's hands gently caressed Ryan's abdominals as he moved down Ryan's body. A kiss fell on the head of Ryan's dick. A tongue licked the shaft. Ryan stared at the cracked plaster in the ceiling as he felt the man apply the slightest suction to ease Ryan's balls into his mouth, where his tongue played across the base of them.

This is ecstasy. This, thought Ryan, is just what I needed.

Ryan felt the man's hands on the inside of his knees. Still with Ryan's balls in his mouth, the man hoisted up Ryan's legs. Ryan's knees bent, his arms still lay limp above his head. Ryan opened his eyes and looked at the man. The man let Ryan's balls flop out of his mouth and gave Ryan a grin. Then he lifted Ryan's legs up farther, spread them, and looked at Ryan's rosebud.

"Beautiful, buddy," the man said.

Ryan smiled.

The man's head bowed. He ducked his head into Ryan's crotch, and then Ryan felt the man's mouth on his hole.

"Oh," growled the man, "So good... So so good."

The sensation, the probing tongue, the warmth of the man's mouth, was a new one to Ryan.

"Omigod. Omigod. That feels great," he said.

Ryan closed his eyes again, enjoying the rim job. His entire body relaxed. After a few minutes of bliss Ryan felt the man's mouth depart and sensed him shift position. He opened his eyes again. The man was on his knees, holding the underside of Ryan's knees in the crook of his elbows. He was grinning at Ryan. Ryan's eyes dropped from his face to his substantial cock. The man was uncut. Ryan had never seen an uncircumcised penis before.

Ryan wanted that big dick inside him. He arched his back. The man cupped one of his hands under his dick and built up spit in his mouth with a few swishes, then spat on his cock, pulled back the thick foreskin, and rubbed the the saliva onto the head.

A synapse fired somewhere in Ryan's brain.

"Wait," he said, "Do you have a condom?"

The man continued to rub the head of his dick.

"No," he answered, "I don't. You got one?"

"No," Ryan answered. Ryan's breath became shallow. He felt a small empty void grow in his lower chest.

"But you want this, right?" asked the man.

"Yeah. Yeah, I do," said Ryan.

"Good boy," said the man. "You're gonna get it sweet boy."

Ryan felt his soul leave his body. He simultaneously looked up at the man, smiling down at him out of the side of his mouth, and also Ryan looked down on the both of them. He felt no fear. He felt nothing. He was only aware of an aching need. He needed to feel the man inside him. He needed to offer himself to the man, completely, holding nothing back. Ryan needed that connection, that intimacy, skin to skin, that only comes with one man fucking another man, the pressure and the losing fight the clenching muscles of the anus put up. Ryan needed to be taken. He needed to be subdued.

Without using his hands, the man positioned his dick against Ryan's hole. Ryan arched his back. He felt himself opening to the man. With no pain, he felt the man's dick ease into him. Their eyes were locked. Ryan noticed that the man's eyes were golden, like amber. He was so handsome. His teeth so white. His full lips were pink. Ryan realized that his lips were the same shade of pink as the head of the man's dick, and he gave a little giggle.

"What?" asked the man.

"Nothing," said Ryan.

Slowly the man's hips started to rock back and forth, his hips started to sway. Like when he was dancing, thought Ryan. He fucks like he dances. Ryan felt the movement inside him. All the way in, all the way out.

Felt so good. So good.

The man increased his tempo. Ryan felt the man's sweat fall on his belly. The man was soaked. He had one eye closed, like a pirate. Ryan guessed because a bead of sweat had trickled into it.

All the way in. All the way out.

So good.

The man increased his tempo still more.

"Uh uh uh," he vocalized.

"Tighten your hole, boy," said the man, "I'm gonna shoot. Milk that load out of me."

Shoot on me, not in me, Ryan thought.

Ryan clenched the muscles in his anus. Immediately he felt the man's dick throb. The man threw back his head and shuddered; his hips spasmed.

He dropped his chin to his chest.

"Whew!" he exclaimed, and laughed.

The man withdrew his softening penis from Ryan. He looked down at it and his smile vanished, replaced by a look of concern.

"Uh oh," he said. He jumped off the bed and ran to the small bathroom. Ryan heard the roll of the toilet paper on the bar. "Yech!" the man said from the bathroom. Then Ryan heard water running in the sink.

The man emerged from the bathroom, drying his crotch with a towel, then using the towel to mop the sweat from his face and head and under his arms.

"I think you're gonna want to clean up, too," the man said. Contracting the muscles in his butt cheeks, Ryan scooted off the bed. As he passed the man on his way around the bed to the bathroom, the man gave him a peck on the cheek and a light slap to his ass.

Ryan sat on the toilet and rolled out some paper. He wiped, examined it, and saw it brown with shit, and drew another length of toilet paper. Wipe. Repeat. Wipe. Repeat. The paper came away clean.

"There's a washcloth there you can use if you need it," the man called from the door.

Ryan decided he didn't need it.

He emerged from the bathroom. They embraced, resting their heads on each other's shoulders.

"Hey, listen," said the man, "I'd ask you to stay, but I have an early day tomorrow." The man glanced at the red numbers on the digital alarm clock sitting on a black plastic milk crate next to the bed. "As a matter of fact," he said laughing, "oh man, my alarm is going to go off in three hours."

He looked at Ryan.

"I'm sorry about that. I shouldn't have gone out tonight." He smiled. "But I'm glad I did."

He kissed Ryan.

"You glad you went out tonight?"

Ryan said he was glad.

The man moved behind Ryan, put his hands on his shoulders, and propelled him out of the bedroom, "Gotta kick you out now," he said.

Ryan collected his clothes. Balancing on one foot and then the other, he put on his socks. Then his t-shirt, then his jeans. He sat on the chair while the man remained standing.

Ryan sat on the chair to put on his boots. The man remained standing.

"Hey," Ryan asked, "so, you're negative, right? With HIV?"

The man didn't move a muscle in his face. His smiled down at Ryan, showing all his white teeth.

"Not sure," said the man. He paused. "But yeah, probably negative."

The smile disappeared. "I doubt you have anything to worry about," and the smile returned.

Again Ryan felt the emptiness in his stomach. His boots back on, he stood. His left leg quivered.

The man said, "Definitely let's do this again." He rooted among the piles on the café table and found a blue ballpoint pen. He tore off the bottom of a sheet of white paper and scribbled something on it. He turned, folded it, and tucked it into the back pocket of Ryan's jeans.

Again a kiss. Ryan did not kiss back.

Ryan rode down in the elevator. The night, or rather very early morning, was still dark, but in the east perhaps a little lighter. Only the occasional cab sped past. Ryan began to shiver. He crammed his hands into his front pockets. He walked south on 8th Avenue, then east on 14th Street. south again on 6th Avenue, then east on 8th Street. He crossed Astor Place and took 7th Street, past the Ukrainian tailors and dress shops, to First Avenue, then south again, crossing Houston.

He shivered all the way home. His mind was blank. Homeless men called to him, asking about spare change. He didn't hear them. A young boy coming the opposite direction on Houston Street veered towards him, and as they passed said, "Pot. Pot. Sinsemilla. Good pot."

Finally, his building. As he fumbled with his keys he realized that his hands were shaking violently. He bit his lip. He suppressed the urge to cry. He would not cry. Nothing to cry about. Everything would be fine. Everything would be fine.

He climbed the stairs, still shivering. Again steadying his shaking hands as he aimed the key at his apartment door. One try. Two tries. Three tries. "Fuck," he said. The key ground into the keyhole. He turned it in the lock, then in the deadbolt (went in first try there) and into his apartment.

There it was. Just as he left it. Still shivering. "Fuck. Why is it so cold."

From a chest of drawers he dug a pair of sweat pants and a sweat shirt. Shivering violently he took off his shirt, then put on the sweatshirt. "So fucking cold," he said out loud. He unbuckled his belt, pulled it through the loops with one motion, and threw it on the floor. He unbuttoned his pants and remembered the paper the man had shoved in his back pocket. Ryan dug out the paper and read what was written there. "Had a great time — hope you did too." No phone number and no name.

Ryan sat on the bed. His shivering subsided. He no longer felt cold. He didn't event know the man's name. He would never know the man's name.

His eyes fell on the thick white piece of expensive card stock with the fine calligraphy that Thales Brice had given him.

New York City • July, 1997

"**Y**ou have two unplayed messages. Playing messages."

"Hi, this is a message for... Mr... Lustig? Mr. Lustig, I'm calling from Westsider Property Management Services. I'm calling to let you know that on Tuesday, due to necessary plumbing work in your building, the water to the building will be shut off at 8 AM in the morning. We expect that service will be restored before 4 PM in the afternoon. This work has to be done, and we apologize for any inconvenience. Thank you."

"Good afternoon. My name is Wilson Chavez. I'm a case manager here at Bailey House. I'm calling at the request of one of our residents, Ryan Sweeney. Mr. Sweeney requested I call you and let you know that he was staying here. If you have any questions, you can call me here at Bailey House between 10 AM and 6 PM, Tuesday through Saturday. The number here is . . ."

Farley didn't hear the number. He had slammed the door behind him and was taking the stairs two at a time.

Ryan sipped water from his plastic cup and looked out the window of the lounge at the Hudson River, glittering in the summer sunlight. He felt bad about declining the invitation to play Trivial Pursuit with three of his fellow inmates. Oscar, who usually was their fourth, had died in the night. But for Ryan, sitting in the sunlight in his wheelchair where the aide had placed him, alone with his thoughts, was the better option.

Seeing the river made him think of Thales. Saturday was the day that he and Thales would leash up the dogs, twin Lhasa Apsos named Rogers and Hart, and walk from their house on Perry Street down to the piers, stopping for iced coffee at the place that Thales felt was the best, leaving the house at

12:30 PM, and getting back before two o'clock. That was on Saturdays when they weren't at the house in Orange County. When they were up at "the farm," that same time slot was given to loading the dogs into the car for a walk at the lake. After the walk, whether along the Hudson or the shores of the lake, Ryan was dispatched to do the grocery shopping while Thales sat at his drafting table listening to recordings of musical theater from the 1910s and 1920s. Ryan looked forward to those shopping trips. With Thales safe at home, he would buy a pack of cigarets and a role of Certs breath mints, making the rounds with his cart to Balducci's, Jefferson Market, Porto Rico Coffee Company down on Christopher Street, and finally the supermarket on Sixth Avenue.

The supermarket.

In addition to being able to smoke, which Thales forbade him to do, the supermarket was the highlight of the Saturday shopping trip. Slowly he would move his cart through the narrow aisles, scrutinizing his list. Almost always his visits coincided with those of "the men." The two men wore identical black one-piece zip-up-the-front tactical uniforms, as were worn by police SWAT teams, and black military jump boots with a high shine. Both men had shaved heads and black goatees. Although one man was slightly taller, the difference in height was not the most important distinguishing characteristic to Ryan's eye. One of the men wore around his neck a length of chain secured with a padlock. He pushed the shopping cart, and when the other man would stop and weigh the relative merits of jars of pasta sauce, he would stop and assume a "parade rest" stance. He wore a neatly folded black bandana in his back right pocket. His counterpart wore the same black bandana, only in his back left pocket.

To the best of Ryan's knowledge they were not aware of Ryan, although he was very much aware of them. On occasion Ryan timed it correctly so that he would be on line for checkout behind them.

The men doing their weekly grocery shopping made Ryan's life so much more difficult than it would have been otherwise.

Ryan had accepted Thales' invitation to dinner and had shown up at his door with a bunch of lilacs he had bought on the way over. (Later Thales had laughingly told him why, with their strong scent, they were an inappropriate choice of blooms to bring to dinner; but, Thales added, "at least you didn't embarrass yourself by a tragic choice of a bottle of undrinkable wine.")

Thales' condominium occupied the top floor of what had been a warehouse. It was, of course, magnificent. Thales was a successful theatrical set designer with the Tony awards to prove it. The fixtures and finishes were shades of deep green and blue. Inside the door was a water feature, a giant Buddha in copper, always glistening and wet from the spout at top of the head, the aqueous murmuring faintly audible throughout the space. Dinner had been a warm salad made with duck and bread and fresh herbs. Ryan had never had duck before. Dessert had been *tiramisu*. ("Trite, I know, but it's a weakness of mine," said Thales.)

After dinner they had sipped espresso and drank brandy and told each other the stories of their lives. Thales had expounded on the virtues of restraint, planning, attention to detail, and nuance, to which he attributed all the success and happiness he had known. His eyelids getting heavy, Ryan had decided to call it a night. Thales had walked Ryan to the door, taken hold of the lapels of his jean jacket, and said, "I would like to ask you to spend the night, but in these situations haste is not the good way to go. I would, however, very much like to see you again."

Ryan came away from that first dinner astonished. What possible interest could Thales Bryce have in him? Thales was handsome and successful. "It caught my eye when I was in Benares," he would say, "there is Hindu symbolism that I don't claim to understand telling the story of the life-giving Ganges River." But off they went together on the following weekend to see a revival of Tennessee Williams' *Summer and Smoke*, and the weekend after that to dinner, and the weekend after that for a stroll along the Promenade in Brooklyn Heights. In spite of his worldliness, Thales had never made Ryan feel like the rube that he was.

Finally Ryan was invited to the house upstate. "I'm having friends of mine up for the weekend and I would very much like you to meet them." The friends turned out to be an actor whose work Ryan very much admired and his partner, who owned an art gallery in Soho. Ryan was excited to meet the actor, although he was quickly disappointed. Ryan had noticed that many successful actors he had had the opportunity to spend time with could not seem to turn it off and were given to odd pronouncements that Ryan recognized as line readings. When Ryan asked for his coffee black, the actor had intoned, "Balzac, you know, died from drinking black coffee."

That first night at the farm Ryan excused himself to smoke on the wide flagstone patio at the back of the house. After a time Thales followed him outside and suggested that rather than spending the night in the guest room, Ryan might spend the night in his room.

Ryan agreed to this arrangement.

And so, after seeing the actor and gallerist off to bed, Ryan and Thales repaired to the master bedroom. After teeth brushing Ryan folded down the antique quilt. After some initial kissing and cuddling, Thales positioned Ryan so he was lying on his side with his feet towards the head of the bed. Thales got himself into position, and the two men performed fellatio on each other. ("Sixty-nine" was the extent of Thales' sexual repertoire.) When both of them had ejaculated, Ryan was sent to the bathroom for washcloths designated for the purpose, made wet with warm water from the sink so they could clean up. Then they went to sleep.

The next morning the gallerist said, "now that you two are 'a couple' . . ." And so Ryan and Thales became a couple. Ryan felt himself to be borne along, as in a canoe without a paddle, floating down a lazy river. The following weekend Thales took Ryan to Barney's ("you have good proportions and you really should wear clothes that fit you correctly") and their purchases were hung in the closet of Thales' condominium on Perry Street. A month later Ryan was dispatched with boxes to clean out his apartment on the Lower East Side. Thales had provided him with twice as many boxes as were needed for his meager possessions, all of which fit in the trunk of a cab.

"This is my partner, Ryan," was how Ryan was introduced to the new circle of friends. "I remember you. You're Thales Bryce's partner, Rob" was what he heard in a chance meeting on the street. The next summer they went to Reykjavik, stopping for a few days in London to see some theater. The summer after that to New Mexico. Then to Brazil and Argentina.

Bryce's world was completely alien to Ryan, as though he had been dragged down to the bottom of the ocean to dwell among the Atlanteans living there in their submerged city. But soon after they had become "a couple," Ryan came to understand that aspects of his life, or what was formerly his life, were unknown to Bryce.

"Let's put our perversions on display for everyone to see," began an angry tirade when two men in leather left the restaurant they were going into. "Let's take our business someplace else. I don't want to be associated with that." Ryan did not contradict Thales then or subsequent times the subject was raised. In a precognitive flash Ryan had carefully folded his leather vest and placed it in a pile of folded sweaters and sweatshirts when he moved into Thales' condominium. There it remained.

Before his second date with Thales, Ryan, at work, had asked a co-worker to clip the padlock of the braided leather collar around his neck. At the time he had told himself that as his Master never removed the lock (although he presumably had the key), Ryan could buy an identical lock the next time he went up to West 80th Street, and the substitution would likely never be discovered. But there had never been a next time.

Sitting in the residents' lounge at Bailey House, the game of Trivial Pursuit proceeding with only three players, Ryan felt his spirit contract remembering this.

He wondered, though, if his life would have been much different had he not let Thales sweep him away to Perry Street.

"You've been careful, haven't you?" asked Thales that first night after dinner. "You're not HIV positive, are you?"

Something in the tone of his voice had indicated to Ryan that he should answer carefully.

"As far as I know I'm not."

This was not a lie. Ryan had never been tested for antibodies to the Human Immunodeficiency Virus. He did not know.

Thales went on to say that had he known that Chip was "infected," he would have felt that he find a more suitable line of work, as the long hours the job entailed may have hastened his decline; and that knowledge, Thales said, was "something he would always have to live with."

Ryan's many talents had made him valued at the company where he worked. Thales thought it fair that their utility bills and condominium association fees be divided proportionally between them, as he thought it would be detrimental to Ryan's sense of self worth if he paid nothing. "You don't want the reputation of being 'kept,' do you?" At the outset, this meant that Ryan's portion was twenty percent, but at the end, it had been forty percent.

Until the end came.

The annual Macy's Thanksgiving Day Parade meant a lot of business for Ryan's company, building many of the floats. This meant long hours producing with a deadline that could not be missed. Ryan attributed his extreme fatigue to the lack of sleep he was getting. He developed a cough that would rack his body — an inconvenient cold. At eleven o'clock on the Sunday night before Thanksgiving, the cough syrup he had been taking had no effect. Had he not been so bleary from the work, he would have realized that his clothes were soaked in sweat. After a fit of coughing he gasped for air as though drowning, unable to catch his breath, then collapsed in front of the armature of the parade float he was making.

The ambulance raced down Seventh Avenue to St. Vincent's Hospital, the scene of his last night with Chip. He woke up in a hospital room, breathing through an oxygen mask. Pneumonia, the doctor told him. And then clarified: pneumocystis carinii pneumonia, referred to by the acronym "PCP." Had he been in treatment the likelihood of contracting this AIDS-defining illness could have been reduced, but Ryan had not been in treatment. His immune system was gone. His viral load was teeming. "Luckily," the doctor had told him, "because your presenting opportunistic infection was PCP, we have a chance."

With Thales, however, Ryan did not have a chance. On his only visit to the hospital, Thales told Ryan he felt betrayed and deceived. Ryan only listened but did not speak. Thales presented Ryan with the address of a storage facility on the West Side Highway, the number of a locker, and a key. Thales had paid for the locker for the next ninety days.

With antibiotics that Ryan swallowed by the fistful, makimg him vomit violently, Ryan recovered from pneumocystis pneumonia. The hospital social worker called Ryan's boss, who wished that there was "something she could do," other than giving him the final paycheck for the hours he had worked and a second check, double the amount of his bi-weekly paycheck. After being discharged, the cheapest motel room he could find in Midtown by the Convention Center quickly depleted this. Rousted by the police for sleeping in the Port Authority Bus Terminal, he was given the address of a shelter. At the shelter, during intake, when he mentioned that he had just gotten out of the hospital, the young woman asked what he had been in for. At the mention of AIDS everything changed. After a night on a cot he was sent to GMHC. That night he spent in a former single-room occupancy hotel, now giving housing to people living with AIDS. There he stayed for the next several weeks. His health deteriorated. He was informed that a bed had been found for him at Bailey House.

His room at Bailey House was cheerful but spare. In the bottom drawer of the desk he found a few scant items belonging to the prior occupant that the cleaning staff had neglected to remove. They consisted to a rolled up poster for The Black Party put on by The Saint-At-Large, a pot pipe, a silver belt buckle made of letters spelling the word "BULLY," and a stack of photographs of men lying naked on a beach. Ryan resigned himself that one day his few possessions would be boxed up and taken away, donated to the Housing Works Thrift Shop. He wondered who would come to wear his leather vest, purchased on Christopher Street, just across Hudson Street from Bailey House.

When he had moved in with Thales, when he and Thales had become a couple, other than an occasional phone call and Christmas cards, he had had no contact with his parents. The thought of contacting them now made him feel exhausted. He didn't doubt that they had already mourned his loss.

But he did want to contact the man whose collar he had worn, the collar that now sat coiled in that same desk drawer. He had given the number to Wilson along with careful instructions on what to say. Wilson had tried to beg off, citing concerns about confidentiality and disclosure, but Ryan had insisted. "He has a right to know," he said.

He could not imagine the man's response, although the phrase "end of a chapter" occurred to him. Perhaps the man had found a new slave. Probably so. Ryan wondered if the branding iron had been used again.

Lost in thought, when he heard the voice, he didn't realize at first that it was not inside his head but vibrating the air of the Bailey House residents' lounge.

"Boy... Ryan."

The Trivial Pursuit players fell silent. Heads turned. There he was. His mustache was now steel gray. He was wearing only jeans and a black t-shirt that said "ALTAR" over his left pectoral. He was still a large man. Ryan remembered how at times, when the man held him, he had felt so small compared to him. Now, skin and bones, the man could easily lift him with one arm.

Shame.

Deep shame.

How had what he had done to Thales been any worse than what Ryan had done to his Master? He had taken his expulsion in stride — aware, perhaps, at the back of his mind, that he was getting his due.

"No," whispered Ryan hoarsely, "No."

The man crossed the room, stood looming over the frail figure in the wheel chair. It seemed to Farley that only the boy's eyes were alive, fitted somehow into a skeleton. Farley could see beneath the thin white skin how Ryan's jawbone connected to his skull.

"Ryan," he said again.

"No," repeated Ryan, "No. I can't... I can't... I thought I could but I can't. I can't. I just wanted to tell you I'm sorry. I'm so sorry." He sobbed. "I didn't mean to. I never..."

"Ryan, boy... You have nothing to be sorry for."

"Yes I do!" shouted Ryan, "and I can never make it up to you! I'm dying, Sir. I'm dying."

Ryan's shouting had brought Bailey house staff into the room. One squatted down next to Ryan, making soothing sounds. A man stood next to Farley, put a tentative hand on his arm, and said, "Maybe it would be better if you come back another time."

Farley docilely let himself be led from the room.

"Sir," called Ryan after him, "I'm so sorry, I'm sorry, Sir."

Southwest Michigan • September, 2003

Farley settled himself on the ground. Although he had been skeptical, he had to admit he was impressed. In the day and a half he had been here he had met men from all over the world: young men, old men. When the "dungeons" were open (the dungeons being a series of large white catering tents), what these men referred to as "the play" was non-stop. Walking through it — the whipping tent, the bondage tent, the raunch tent, down across the parking lot to the "noisy dungeon" in a barn-like structure, everywhere were men practicing ancient rites. Men were bound and suspended, archipelagos of hypodermic needles without the syringes patterned men's torsos, every sling was taken as fingers tickled the nether reaches of men's bowels, the air was filled with the slap of floggers and the crack of whips and the moans and grunts of the men on whom they landed.

Farley, although he had been told to "make his own fun," was content to watch, politely declining invitations to "play" or evading questions about what he was "into." His purpose in coming here, driving a day and a half across five states, was solitary: Farley was here to get what he had coming to him.

Since he had said goodbye to Ryan, or rather since Ryan had said goodbye to him, he had been emptied out, extinguished. Grief and Regret and Sorrow followed him like phantoms, tracing his steps, and at odd moments, for odd reasons, they would make their presence known. Sometimes he would cry. Sometimes he would find a place to sit, close his eyes, and let the images and memories of Ryan proceed through his imagination like the vision of the Kings of Scotland in Macbeth. There was Ryan entering the bar so long ago. How splendid he had looked. Like a magnificent young warrior, fresh from the battlefield, pushing through the door of some medieval tavern. Had Ryan been aware that at the moment he had entered, he had made the bar his own? The men in the bar, Farley included among them, had not begun to live until Ryan had brought them to life.

When Farley had seen Ryan, it was as though his life, flailing, random, and serendipitous, was suddenly given purpose. I want to destroy him, Farley had said to himself, to destroy him and thereby save him.

Ages ago that Swedish psychiatrist with the forgotten name had drawn on his pipe, let the smoke fall from his lips, and said, "Before you begin to live, you must commit suicide."

He went on to explain that from the cradle we are saddled with the expectations of others. The bit in our mouth and the bridle is "who we are supposed to be." We accept this without question, and many men go on to live shallow and empty lives, only in the middle of insomniac nights wondering where they had gone wrong, what signpost overgrown with shrubbery they had missed.

There would be none of that for that handsome young man who strode into the Eagle and lit a cigaret. Farley would see to that.

Farley would strip everything away from him, return him to a primordial animal state, let him glimpse within himself a powerful will to live and the courage and strength to do so. And then, when the boy was raw and bloodied, Ryan would free him by locking a collar around his neck. Within the circle of that collar the boy would discover himself for the first time. With Farley's subjugating hand resting on his head as he knelt, the boy would send roots down deep into the soil beneath them, learn to draw his energy from the earth itself, and from the wintry ground of oblivion, something new would grow, Ryan but not Ryan. It would grow strong and tall and would bear fruit.

But that was not to be.

Ryan's phone calls had become irregular, and then stopped. At the time Farley had believed that their bond was so strong that although it could be frayed by the usual vicissitudes of a young man's life, it would not be broken. He would wait. Wait for the boy to return, and then they would pick up where they had left off.

His mistake was not realizing that the tether had been too long. It had not been enough for Farley to sit stoically in his lair, almost anonymous, becoming for the boy his erotic ideals and the object of his deepest longings and deepest fears that he must face made flesh.

The boy had needed him to play Polonius, to guide and to forbid.

Farley shunned this. Surely that would destroy the magic they had kindled together. Surely their time together, when time stopped moving forward and the world seemed to hold its breath, surely that would be enough.

And now Farley had come here to to this gathering because he needed to be destroyed. His roots needed to go deeper down into the firmament, deep enough to draw sustenance, entwined with the roots of other men, both those living, out there digging deeper around him on the crosses and in the slings, and those who had gone before and those who were yet to come. The thin skin of soil that covers the earth, where men are buried, for which wars are fought, from which new life springs, it also exists outside of time.

He had become aware of a need to reconnect, but the knowledge of to what was slower in coming. And he still did not know. But what he was sure of was that before that could happen, he must atone. He must make atonement for having failed Ryan. Farley didn't believe such a thing was possible; a true and complete atonement would surely be beyond any ordeal. Nothing would bring Ryan back from the midnight kingdom of the shades where he now dwelt. But he knew that he must try.

And he knew the man he would make priest in this sacrament.

He had remembered the man from those evenings in the loft apartment. During dinner conversation was conducted in murmurs and whispers. The night's events would be different. Ralph was here. Farley had looked down the table at the man, sitting in the place of honor to the right of the host, laughing with gusto at some joke the host had made to him.

Ralph was a large man, almost as large as Farley, and adorned with a similar bushy mustache. To the left of the host sat a square-jawed German visitor, lithe and muscular. The German's nervousness was palpable. He pushed his food around on his plate, letting the naked footman take away almost as much as he had served him.

After dinner they had risen from the table and proceeded in silence to the large drawing room, Ralph and the German in the lead.

With a long, thick whip, Ralph had whipped the German. For a time the German had stood stretched on the cross as though he were carved from wood, like a gladiator undergoing training. But then, first with a few involuntary yelps and then with a cascade of cries, he had broken. Ralph continued his assault. The German hammered the cross as best he could with the wrist restraints; he threw back his head and bellowed.

His upper back, across his broad shoulders and down his *latissimus dorsi*, was scarlet with his blood, which flowed stickily downwards, over the twin mounds of his buttocks, down his sturdy thighs, the rivulets gathering as they found their way down his calves as tributaries form rivers.

Ralph continued to swing the long black bullwhip until something told him that it was finished. He had gone to where his gear sat in a neat pile and drawn from the pile a black leather blanket, an entire cowhide. With that over his shoulders, he had first knelt on one knee behind the still-bound German, just for a moment, in what Farley had been sure was a brief, silent homage. Then, before rising, he unbuckled the black leather restraints around the German's ankles, then stood upright and did the same with the wrist restraints. The German's shoulders heaved in spasms although he was silent. Then Ralph stretched out his arms under the cowhide, looking like dark wings unfurled. Ralph pressed his chest against the German's bloody back, closed his arms and the cape around the boy, and in this leather tent both of them collapsed slowly to the floor.

That was what Farley wanted.

He had trouble tracing Ralph. But luckily, although he had not been a regular at those nights in the loft, the memory of what they had witnessed had not faded in the minds of the men who had witnessed it. Farley sought out those men, all too frequently getting the news that they were dead, news that stabbed him like a knife every time he received it. He worried that Ralph may be among the fallen. Ralph had been in town from Seattle. Finally one of the men who had been a footman that night had the information he had sought: Ralph Bristow. Yes, he had lived in Seattle, but now he had retired to Palm Springs.

Directory Assistance had one Ralph Bristow with a Palm Springs address. Farley gulped down the last of his glass of good Scotch whiskey and dialed the number.

In an almost incoherent torrent, as soon as he had confirmed that this was the man he sought, he tried his best to convey what it was he wanted. Ralph said he understood.

"Should I come to you? How soon could I come?"

Ralph Bristow thought and then said, "This cannot be a private event. What you have done has separated you from all of us. You must make your peace not only with the boy, but with your brothers. There will be witnesses."

Farley had received an invitation to the event at Ralph's request. He had filled out the form and sent it off with his check. He had received his confirmation letter with the news that as all men attending had to perform volunteer service during the three days, he would be assigned latrine duty.

Ralph was well known among these men. He had a cloud of hopeful suitors following him from among whom he selected a lucky few. He told Farley that the last night, Saturday, he had set aside for their rite.

Farley could not bring himself to engage with any of the other men in the meantime. The memories evoked would be too painful. When he was not at dinner or cleaning and mopping out the bathrooms, he stayed in his shared room. He had found that wandering the grounds of the resort made men seek him out. Instead he had found a patch of earth at a slight remove from the activity and would sit there on the ground, impassive and sphinx-like, as was his lifelong habit.

His first thought waking up on Saturday morning was that this was the appointed day. He went to breakfast late after most of the men had cleared out of the mess and sat alone. Lunch he ate sitting in his spot under the tree. At one point Ralph, leading a lucky man towards the whipping tent, let his solemn gaze fall on Farley and slowly nodded a greeting. Farley ate little at dinner, although this was purported to be the finest fare of the weekend; but he downed three glasses of wine.

After dinner it was announced that the dungeons were open. Farley saw Ralph, shirtless and wearing tight black leather breeches. "I'll be waiting for you in the noisy dungeon in half an hour," he said; then he walked away. Farley left the mess, went back to his quarters, drew a cigar from his shirt pocket, and enjoyed it while he strolled through the compound. His perambulations brought him to the noisy dungeon. At the far end Ralph and the heavy wooden St. Andrew's cross were waiting for him.

Without speaking a word Ralph indicated to Farley to remove the black sweatshirt he wore. Farley peeled off his shirt, and Ralph proceeded to circle Farley where he stood, sizing him up. Then Farley felt the man's hands massaging his back and chest and arms.

"You've got a good thick hide on you, boy," Ralph said.

"Yes, Sir," said Farley. Ralph applied the black leather wrist restraints, not looking up from his work. With the restraints in place, Ralph led Farley towards the waiting cross. One step away Farley stopped, turned towards Ralph, then dropped to his knees and kissed each of the man's boots. "Thank you, Sir," Farley said.

Ralph made no reply.

Farley stepped forward and leaned against the cross, took a deep breath, and stretched out his arms. Ralph secured Farley's wrists to the cross with carabiner clips. Farley bowed his head.

By arrangement there would be no "warm up." This would be a whipping pure and simple. Ralph would whip him and Farley would take it.

A deep silence followed. Farley took another deep breath.

He started slightly at the loud crack of the bullwhip behind him. He set his feet, grounding himself, feeling the earth beneath his feet.

Behind Farley, Ralph gracefully swung the whip out behind him. For an instant it hung in the air, extended its full length, parallel to the ground. Then, as gracefully, Ralph brought the whip forward.

The fine nylon strands at the end of the braided black leather bullwhip connected with the meat of Farley's back, and the crack seemed to echo throughout all of Creation. However painful Farley imagined it would be to be whipped, the pain he felt was greater.

He steeled himself, but then saw the way forward clearly... No. He would hold nothing back. Nothing at all. He would offer himself completely to this man. He tilted back his head.

When the next throw of the whip connected, Farley began to weep. The falls kept coming. The pain did not diminish, but each land seemed to elide with the one before it and the one after it. Farley continued to weep. And then he thought of Ryan, naked, on his knees, hands crossed at the wrist behind his back. He thought of Ryan strapped down to the fuck bench, so still with the stillness that comes from deep submission as Farley had retrieved the branding iron from the kitchen, it's end glowing like a beacon. Now Ryan was on the floor among the sawdust and crushed beer cans in fetters and manacles that night at the Mineshaft. How perfect the boy had looked.

And then he also saw the round, sunburned face of Private Johnson. Somewhere a mother had opened an envelope with a Department of Defense return address and read the news that she would never see her son alive again. The enormity of what he had done, so carelessly and cruelly, made Farley heave great sobs. This was another sin for which he would never be able to atone.

The ground beneath him seemed to vanish. Farley felt himself falling down, down, down, deeper and deeper into the earth. The sound of the bullwhip cracking became fainter and fainter, farther and farther away. The surface became a distant memory. Now that was far above him. His chest convulsed. Farley cried, he wailed, as he had never cried before. He became a creature of grief, buried in sorrow; loss and loneliness choked him. Each time the whip fell he would let out a hoarse scream. His throat was raw; tears streamed from his eyes until his ducts were empty reservoirs. Still he descended, deeper and deeper. Surely soon he would come crashing through the ceiling of Hell. If there was not a Hell, then he would continue falling forever.

Something, something was calling to Farley, calling him back to his body. He opened his eyes. Ralph had squirmed between the cross and the wall it leaned on; his face was inches from Farley's.

"It is done," said Ralph.

Farley realized he no longer felt the whip on his back. He seemed to be vibrating, floating. But then he understood: he no longer felt the pain from the whipping, but he felt a greater pain, a pain that was all his, uncreated and eternal, with him always. Again he fell into sobs.

He sobbed as Ralph let his hands free from the restraints. He sobbed as Ralph turned him around. Farley collapsed into Ralph's arms, sobbing all the while.

They lowered themselves to the floor, Ralph leaned back against one leg of the cross, Farley buried his face in Ralph's furry, firm chest and cried for all he was worth.

The storm of Farley's anguish gradually stilled. When the capacity to form words returned to him, he said again, "Thank you, Sir."

After a time, Ralph separated himself from Farley and rose to his feet, then hauled Farley up. Arm in arm they walked away from the cross. Ralph nodded to his boy who had been standing silently by, the signal for his boy to pack up Ralph's gear and clean up after them.

Farley became aware that men were standing silently in a semi-circle. There was no other play going on in the barn. The men parted to let Ralph and Farley pass. Ralph paused to grab two bottles of water from a mini-fridge just inside the door, and they walked out into the night, not speaking, still arm in arm. Now and then Farley would heave a sigh, and Ralph would hold him a little tighter. Ralph passed one of the bottles of water to Farley. Farley downed it in one gulp, feeling it soothe his throat, raw from screaming.

They came to a picnic table in the darkness. Farley sat at one side, Ralph at the other. The two men faced each other.

"Now," Ralph said, "can you go on?"

Palm Springs, California • February, 2017

Consciousness blossomed, dreams faded and were replaced by first sounds (the snoring of his Master), then sensation (the cold steel around his ankles, wrists, and neck). Ryan opened his eyes. His position on the floor gave him a view across the carpet. He stretched his limbs to the extent that his chains allowed him to. As noiselessly as he could he raised himself on all fours, then crawled to the foot of the bed. He surveyed the terrain. His Master slept on his back, and this morning his legs were spread wide, making it easy for Ryan to navigate. He raised his head and shoulders onto the bed, drew back the blanket, and walking on his elbows made his way towards his objective.

His Master's dick lay like a sleeping bird. Gently and slowly Ryan got himself into position. It was important to him that the first sensation he gave his Master was his slave's mouth on his dick.

Success.

He kissed it, then opened his mouth and swallowed the head and the soft body of it, sucking slightly until it all sat in his warm mouth. His Master's snoring abated. "Mmm," he said, and his member started to fill with blood.

Ryan received it to the back of his mouth and then down his throat as it swelled. Then he gently pulled back, feeling his mouth fill with saliva, then took it in. His Master didn't stir. His eyes remained closed.

Ryan worked for some time before Farley inhaled deeply. Here it comes, Ryan thought.

The piss began to flow, filling his mouth. He opened his throat to give it an outlet, breathing deeply through his nose. The stream reduced to a trickle. Ryan kept his mouth still until he was sure he had gotten every drop. Then he eased himself off the bed, crawled around to the side, and assumed the position, kneeling, head bowed.

"Sir, thank you, Sir," he said.

His Master raised himself up on his elbows, reached over and grabbed a key on a loop of thin leather from the nightstand on the other side of the bed from where his slave knelt. (Ryan would not be able to reach it without crawling across his sleeping Master.) Ryan moved himself forward. His Master inserted the key into the padlock that connected his steel collar to a chain that ended in an eyebolt in the wall behind the bed. His Master placed the padlock and key on the nightstand and then grumbled, "Oatmeal. With raisins. Do we have apples? Then with an apple. Cut up. Coffee. Make sure it's hot this morning, boy."

Ryan rose to his feet, his chains clinking. Without turning his back on his Master he backed out of the bedroom. Once through the door he exited the casita—two rooms and a bathroom— that sat at the back of his Palm Springs home. He rounded the pool and entered his house through the glass sliding doors.

Ryan's boy Sully, wearing gym shorts, was up and busy in the kitchen, getting his own breakfast going.

Sully wished his Daddy a good morning. "Got the coffee going already."

Ryan thanked him.

He selected an apple from the bowl on the countertop, got the oatmeal and raisins from the pantry, and set to work.

Ryan had collared Sully three years previously. His boy was the reason he had been in Palm Springs that October weekend a year and a half before. Sully had won a contest in a bar in Los Angeles where they both had been living at the time and gone on to be First Runner-Up in the Mr. LA Leather Contest. As a newly minted "leader in the leather community," Sully had felt himself obligated to get out and wear his sash. And so he had convinced his Daddy that they should be in Palm Springs the last weekend in October to attend the Mr. Palm Springs Leather Contest.

Ryan had endured the weekend, the contest, the pool parties, the formal leather dinner, with good humor. Other than what the attendees were wearing, he couldn't figure out what in particular made it "leather." Surely librarians, microbiologists, and retired merchant seamen at their gatherings had the same mix of entertainment and diversions. "Leather has probably changed a lot since you were my age," Sully had counseled.

Indeed it had. Mostly. Some elements seem to hang on. Including leathermen gathering to drink beer and smoke cigars. On Sunday afternoon of Palm Springs Leather Pride Weekend, Sully and Ryan had gone to the Barracks for the "victory party" that concluded the weekend. The bar, a barn-like space with a large patio surrounded by stockade fencing, was packed.

Sully found a group of his fellow titleholders, whom he referred to as "my brothers," and Ryan left them to compare notes on the contest and the new Mr. Palm Springs Leather. After a long wait at the bar, he got himself a beer and then squirmed through the crowd, making his way to the patio. Men were clustered in groups. Ryan nodded to a few of the guys he knew from Avatar. He thought his chances of finding someplace to sit would be better at the periphery, so he made his way for the corner.

The crowds parted as if in a movie musical, and Ryan saw him. His beer slipped from his hand, the bottle breaking, spattering the boots of the men standing near him and his old worn Redwings. Ryan was oblivious to their protests and dirty looks. On a bench against the fence next to the bootblack chair sat Farley Lustig, his head tilted in conversation with the man sitting next to him. Stumbling as though drunk, Ryan made his way forward. Farley was making some point to the man he was speaking with, jabbing his cigar towards the man, emphasizing a point. The man noticed Ryan's approach before Farley did.

Ryan dropped to his knees in front of Farley. The man Farley was speaking to asked, "Now who is this?"

"This," said Farley, "is my slave."

With his California State Contractor's license, Ryan had found it easy to move to Palm Springs from Los Angeles. Sully, who worked in video production, found a small video production company that agreed to take him on part time, and he supplemented this by working as a trainer at a local gym.

When the new owner of the building where Farley lived made it clear that he intended to clear out the tenants and renovate, he had taken an early retirement from the Federal Reserve Bank of New York and decided to move to the Desert, sharing a house with Ralph Bristow, with whom he had developed a close friendship.

Everything had fallen into place quickly and easily. Sully had taken the change in his relationship with his Daddy in stride. He was not sure if his Daddy's Master had ever learned his name. He was addressed as "boy" and the older man seemed to take it for granted that anyone he gave an order to would carry out that order. But from their first meeting, when Sully had returned from the Barracks to find Ryan and Farley in a tearful embrace in the room at the resort he and his Daddy had occupied that weekend, he knew that this relationship was something that he and everyone else in the world could only look upon with wonder.

Sully and Ryan had met when Sully had been working on a project called "Lazarus," interviewing men living with AIDS who, in the mid-nineties, had been dying when Highly Active Anti-Retrovirus Therapy, or HAART, had seemingly miraculously restored them to health. Through the lens of his camera Sully couldn't imagine that the soft-spoken but assured man with his sturdy frame and pelt of blond hair on his tanned chest had at one time been told that all available treatments had failed, his life was a matter of months if not weeks, and so there was little to lose by trying this unproven combination of powerful drugs. Ryan had seemed embarrassed by the attention.

"Did your life go back to the way it had been before you got sick?" the interviewer asked.

For the first time in the interview, Ryan had teared up. "No," he answered simply, "I had lost everything."

Sullly now understood that the "everything" that Ryan referred to was Farley Lustig.

"Sul'…" Ryan glanced at his Master. "Slave," he began again, "Would you please give us a few hours? Maybe hang out by the pool?" on the night of the reunion at the Barracks.

Sully, tired after the long weekend, had thought to take a nap on one of the lounge chairs around the pool. There would be no nap. For the next two hours, he and the other guests of the resort were treated to a symphony of the sounds of Farley's broad belt slapping against Ryan's body, Farley's barked commands ("You're gonna stand there and take it, boy!"),

Ryan's yelps and hollers, all of this punctuated by both of their hysterical, joyous laughter. After the belting reached its crescendo, the fucking started, Ryan singing a new song of gratitude and exaltation. Finally the door had opened. Farley emerged first, fully clothed, followed by Ryan, stark naked except for his Redwings, his body covered in deep red welts.

Farley turned. Ryan stopped.

"Slave!" barked Farley.

"Sir, this slave will report at your quarters at 0900, Sir!"

"See that you do, slave."

With Sully sitting on the bed and Ryan pacing (it was still too painful for him to sit down), the story came pouring out of Ryan. At one point, overcome with the memories, Sully was dispatched to buy a box of Marlboro Reds for his Daddy. When Sully returned he found Ryan weeping.

"Do you know what he said to me? I didn't think he'd take me back, not after what I had done to him. But he pointed to this... did I ever show you this?" Ryan indicated the mark on his right butt cheek that Sully had always taken to be a birthmark or a scar. "This is where he branded me. And he said, 'This means that you are my property, boy. For good.' He's heading to Home Depot to buy a padlock and some chain. I still have the collar—his collar—at home back in LA, but the chain will do until he can put it on me again himself and lock it in place."

Farley Lustig sat out by the pool, eating his oatmeal and drinking the good hot coffee his slave had brought him. His slave would be away for the day, busy with a job down in Palm Desert. When the boy returned after his morning at the gym where he worked, it would be the boy who drove him to the Veteran's Administration hospital in Loma Linda and brought him home again.

Farley winced at the thought. On the last trip to Loma Linda all manner of tests had been performed by his young doctor, Dr. Lao. He swallowed more coffee. The young woman was Laotian, but her features suggested to Farley his time in Vietnam, a time that was still painful to remember.

Why, Farley wondered, was Palm Springs not swarming with painters? The light here was like none other. It was golden and seemed to turn everything it fell on to gold, too. An artist could spend his life trying to capture that golden light on canvas.

Everything, indeed, was golden.

Farley had been right. The bond between him and his slave had been unbreakable. Even death, in a way, had failed to sever it. The bond had been forged that first night they met, when Farley had given the boy all he could dish out, holding nothing back, not wanting to dishonor the boy's strength and courage with his tentativeness. And time and time again the bond was tempered in their encounters. The depths of his slave's devotion and obedience were unfathomable, without limit, although Farley never grew tired of seeking out those limits. Ryan's submission had demanded of him his very best. Sometimes he had wondered if the boy would exhaust Farley's supply of whatever ancient power used him as its vessel when he beat the boy. Surely Ryan would raise his bowed head and see that Farley was, after all, just a man, as plagued by fear and insecurity and frustration and pettiness as any man. But something in the alchemy of their interplay molded Farley perhaps more than it did Ryan. From the first he felt he must be worthy of the boy. He felt called to turn the base elements of who he was into something more, something greater than human. When he had made Ryan his slave, his journey began in becoming a Master. Farley's end had been his beginning.

It nearly destroyed him when Ryan had drifted away. When the night would pass without a call from the boy, every minute was a hectoring intimation that he had failed at the one defining task of his life. And when the call did come and he had raced downtown, pleading with the cab driver to go faster, finding Ryan sitting there in a wheelchair, he knew that the labor the gods had set before him had proven to be beyond him. He was a failed hero.

But what was this? A second chance? It didn't feel like that to Farley. No. That descent into Hell had been part of his odyssey. For now, with no flicker of doubt, the boy was his slave, completely and absolutely and for all time, and he was the Master of a man. Not just any man: a strong, wise, beautiful, and courageous man. A great man. It was a great man who wore his collar. Ryan was a great man, and he was mastered completely.

"Are you ready to go, Sir?"

Ah. The boy was back.

This boy, he reflected, was indeed a boy. He didn't know who he was. He didn't know what he wanted. Was Ryan the one who would teach him? Farley thought not. Not because of any deficit on Ryan's part. The boy was not ready to learn. Perhaps, Farley sighed, he never would be.

"We better get a move on, boy."

Farley was quiet on the way back from Loma Linda. He asked Sully ("We don't need that radio right now") to silence the radio. Sully paid attention to traffic on the Ten Freeway. Construction outside of Yucaipa slowed them to a crawl. Farley took advantage of the slowdown, rolled the passenger side window down, and lit a cigar.

"Sully," he said—Sully startled, hearing himself addressed by his name for the first time by the old man—"Do you believe yourself to be destined for greatness?"

The silence continued. Just when Farley was wondering if the boy was not going to reply at all, Sully said, "I'm not sure what you mean, Sir. I think I want what all of us want. I want a comfortable home, I want friends, I'd like to travel some. I have family in Ireland I've never met."

"But you feel no call to greatness? To heroism?"

"You mean, like joining the military, Sir? I think I'm too old. Unless we had a war. And then I don't know if I'd want that."

They rode on in silence. After a time Farley decided on another approach.

"I believe you are capable of doing great things. You have the capacity for greatness. But the challenge before you is to discover that capacity within you. Most men never do. They take the safe path, they live lives of caution, they hide in the crowd.

"You should make your way to the deep end of the pool. Then just jump in. Find a risk to take, one that you're not sure that you will survive. Once you conquer your fears, once you come face to face with your own mortality, then you will realize that there is nothing you have to be afraid of. Then you'll be free, boy."

Sully didn't offer a response. Farley did not demand one. The pace of traffic returned to normal. Farley let his cigar go out and rolled up the window.

Congestive Heart Failure. Doctor Lao had explained it thoroughly to him. If there was a good response to treatment, progress could be slowed. But his heart just was not able to do the work it had once done, sending the blood coursing through his arteries, delivering oxygen to all the cells in his body. As a result it would work harder and harder, and more and more of the tasks of daily living would prove to require exertion.

Farley had taken this with equanimity. But then what she had said chilled him: many people with congestive heart failure experience cognitive difficulties as the brain is deprived of the oxygen it needs. He may become forgetful and confused.

"Not that," thought Farley. His sphere of operations getting smaller and smaller — that he could live with. But not sinking slowly into a foggy pit of unknowing. Not his mind. Not that.

The work with his slave: he wondered if that was complete. He felt that it was. There was little more that he could offer the boy. Although... In a flash, Farley saw the way forward. That would be his gift to his slave. His slave had offered up to him his body, his mind, and his spirit. In return, he would give to his slave everything he had left to give.

The Southern California
Desert • June, 2017

"**H**ere's the road where we turn, boy."

Ryan slowed and put on his blinker, turning off a four-lane state highway onto a two-lane county highway.

Ryan's Master and his Master's friend Ralph had been poring over roadmaps out by the pool. Ryan had suggested to Ralph—Ryan would not have offered any suggestion unsolicited to his Master, not that his Master had ever in almost forty years solicited Ryan's opinion on anything—that with an address or even with longitude and latitude, he could set the GPS on his phone to take them to wherever they were going.

"As you were, slave," had been the answer from his Master, and Ryan had gone back to cleaning the pool. They had told their pool man that his services were no longer needed because his Master had decided he liked to watch his muscular slave, naked and sweating in the afternoon sun, cleaning the pool. 'Seeing as we don't have crops you can tend to, slave."

The appointed day had come. After a big breakfast Ryan had loaded Farley's big black canvas duffle bag into the trunk, along with enough liter bottles of water in a number that Ryan thought would be sufficient, although he didn't know where they were going and didn't know what they would be doing when they got there.

After Sully's departure two month's prior, all the work of housekeeping had fallen to him. This he didn't mind. Although he sometimes smiled at the fact that beds in the two bedrooms in the house never needed to be made or the bedclothes changed as his Master had continued to live in the casita out back, and every night Ryan slept in chains on the mat on the floor next to his Master's bed, his head resting on the toes of his Master's empty boots.

Sully had announced that he was going back to LA, giving as his reason dissatisfaction with the opportunities for growth offered by the video production company he worked for. Sully's Daddy had treated him to a farewell dinner at the boy's favorite restaurant and helped him load up his belongings into the back of his SUV. A month later an email from his boy showed up in his inbox. Ryan opened it and was surprised to read that Sully was headed to Uzbekistan to teach English with a British non-governmental organization.

"Pay attention to the miles, boy. Count them off to me," his Master had ordered.

"One, Sir. One mile."

"Two, Sir."

When he counted twelve, he was ordered to slow down. Finally his Master told him to pull off the road. "Keep the two left tires on the asphalt, boy."

"Sir, yes Sir!"

Ryan hauled the heavy duffle bag from the back of the car. He presented one of the bottles of water to his Master, then took one for himself. Four more he put in a satchel, which he slung over his shoulder.

By now it was almost noon. The sun baked the desert around them. The blooms of February and March were long gone. The dry, skeletal ocotillo looked dead, although, of course, they were not — just dormant, waiting until the rains came again, however briefly, until they turned from gray to bright green and sent out beautiful red blooms at the end of their branches.

But now all was desolation. The pitiless sun in the cloudless blue sky overhead, the ashen wastes of the Great Sonoran Desert around them. It was an existential landscape, stripped to bleakness, nothing superfluous: except for them, the only things living and breathing that were evident.

Hoisting the two bags on his shoulders, Ryan was ready for the last part of the journey.

"My beast of burden," said his Master, and gave one of his rare smiles, that smile that made Ryan feel to the core of his being that all was right with the world and he was the most fortunate man who had ever lived, to enjoy the protection and ownership of a Master like none other.

"Yes, Sir! Your beast of burden, Sir!" he said, and gave his Master a grin in return.

His Master surveyed the landscape and headed away from the roadway down an embankment. His beast of burden shambled after him, grunting with the effort, taking careful steps over the loose sand.

They descended into a bone-dry arroyo, then climbed the hill on the opposite side. His Master reached the top first, put his hands on his hips, and said aloud to no one (certainly not to his slave): "There it is. Just where he said it would be."

A few minutes later, when Ryan reached the top, he saw his Master descending the other side and knew at once what he was heading for. The hill they had just summited was a ridge running parallel to the roadway, and the ridge sheltered a small valley, about twice the size of a football field, before the desert rose up again on the other side. In roughly the center of the depression was a granite outcropping, smoothed and rounded by eons of wind and sand. To Ryan it looked like a gigantic fingertip. He imagined the graven image of some old god, sculpted to a monstrous and monumental scale so as to inspire awe and fear in the people who worshipped it, buried and forgotten under the sand.

The southern face sloped upwards at about a sixty degree angle. His Master indicated to Ryan to drop the duffle bag and the water in the shadow of the overhang of the northern aspect of the solid granite rock. His Master bent over the duffle bag, opened it, and drew from it a flogger, one Ryan had never seen before. The tails were an inch and a half wide and a quarter inch thick. From the handle to the tips of the tails must have measured five feet. Using both hands, his Master took a few tentative swings. Ryan noted that the flogger was well made. As it swung, the the tails all stayed together, no stragglers. "He must have borrowed it from Ralph Bristow," Ryan thought.

His Master tossed the flogger over one shoulder so equal weight fell down his chest and down his back. In a gesture that surprised Ryan so much that for several seconds he stood stock still, his Master opened up his arms. Head bowed, the slave moved forward and was enfolded tenderly in the arms of his Master in an embrace. His Master's hands tenderly stroked the back of the slaves head and neck, running the short blond curly hair through his meaty fingers, the other hand gently moving up and down the slave's spine from buttocks to shoulders. His Master's massive torso heaved—the slave, wondering, realized his Master was crying—and then his Master quickly composed himself.

"To whom much has been given, much is expected," the Master whispered in his slave's ear. "I have given you all I had to offer. And now the golden gift is in you. You must go out into the world and find someone on whom you can bestow it."

For the first time in all of his experiences as a slave Ryan felt fear. He could not imagine the import of these words. He did

not have long to turn them over in his mind. The familiar hand at the nape of his neck guided him in an about-face to the south face and forward until his feet could go no further at the base of the protrusion. "Legs spread, arms out," came the order.

Ryan got himself into position. His Master's beefy hand in the center of his back pushed him forward and off balance. He fell against the slope of the granite. He gave a yelp: the rock was hot as a griddle from the desert sun. He stifled himself. It was unworthy of the Master who owned him that he should notice pain.

Soon he heard the swoosh of the enormous black flogger as his Master swung it through the air, sounding like the wings of some huge bird of prey swooping just past him. He felt the rush of hot air against the skin of his back. He quieted his mind and waited. He did not wait long.

When the flogger fell, it was the power of the throw rather than the pain he felt that resonated. This flogger, inexpertly used, could break bones. But it would not break Ryan. He gave a growl and let the muscles of his back expand. With equal parts gratitude and determination to show his Master how much his slave could take, Ryan smiled as the assault built in ferocity. The pain intensified, and when the tails of the flogger struck him, Ryan began to hear a slapping sound. He knew from experience what this meant. The assault had sent his blood rushing to the surface of his skin, a criss-cross of thick red welts had risen. As the falls continued to rain on his back, his white blood cells had seeped through the epidermis, lying slick and greasy. Soon the tenderized skin would break from the blows. Once again he would bleed for the man who owned him.

Ryan was grateful for the setting his Master had chosen for this rite. His arms were outstretched on the rocky extension of the granite bedrock, the bones of the earth. Between the earth and the sky with the midday sun overhead there was only him. He and the man swinging the flogger were alone on the planet, alone in the universe. All the energy of the Cosmos flowed between slave and Master, Master and slave. In every instant, they were created and destroyed and recreated. Once again they had stepped outside of time.

Like a kite reeled in, Ryan's consciousness shrank to the pin-point of his skull once again. Something was different, something had changed. He realized that the beating had ceased. He closed his eyes and waited. Beyond the sound of the blood rushing through his ears, the desert offered only silence, no rustle of wind, no birdsong. Ryan waited, breathing deeply. He slowly raised his head from the granite pillow. Silence. He flattened his palms against the hot rock and raised his body. Silence still. He extended one arm, twisting his body, turning his head to look behind him.

Farley Lustig lay face down in the sand, the heavy flogger still held tight in his hand.

Palm Springs, California • April, 2019

This, thought Micah, is a Thing. "A Thing" was the term Micah used with his therapist, Jen, to describe events in his life where the path his life was going to take pivoted and all of a sudden he was set on a new course.

Micah discovered that even flexing his muscles and shifting his weight brought no motion. With few preliminaries after Micah had arrived after the drive up from San Diego, Ryan ordered him to strip and to help him get into the bondage suit. The suit was made of heavy black leather, a one-piece that zipped up the back, the exterior covered in straps that had been tightened and many, many D-rings. After he was in he found that the leather was so thick that his movements were restricted as he sat on the floor to put his boots back on. He felt himself getting hard with this discovery. Boots on, he stood again, and the Man started tightening the straps, making the suit more restrictive still. A wooden chair was placed in the middle of an armature made from connected steel pipe. Micah was instructed to kneel on the chair facing backwards, his chest towards the chair back. When he was in place, the Man put on the leather hood. It was tight, and as buckles were buckled running up the back, it got tighter. The only holes in the hood were two grommets where it lay over his nostrils. There was no light, and sound was muffled. The Man guided his hands into mitts, leather without fingers or a thumb, and these, too, were buckled in place. Finally, a thick, padded leather collar was pressed about his neck. More working of buckles. Then, for nearly an hour (although Micah had lost track of the passage of time soon after he was encased head to toe in leather), the Man worked with ropes, threading them through the D-rings and tying them off to the overhead cross pieces of the steel frame. Rope was additionally woven between the D-rings on the arms and legs of the bondage suit, immobilizing him.

Finally, the sensation of the ropes ceased. Micah was only able to wiggle his fingers slightly in the leather mitts. The only physical sensation that Micah felt was the hard wooden chair underneath his knees. Then, with some rocking to get the feet over the lower cross pieces of the frame, Micah was suspended motionless in space, like a black leather fly caught in the middle of a spider's web of rope.

"If you're thinking," said the Man, "that this isn't going to be painful, think again. Your muscles are going to start to cramp, and there is nothing that you can do about it. And if you piss in my bondage suit, after I whip you until you bleed, you will be down on your knees taking care of the leather while I continue to whip you. So hold it in."

Yes, definitely this was a Thing.

This was the last thing that could be described as "a thought" that passed through Micah's head. Without the input of sound, light, smell, or sensation, the boy's mind drifted through a series of vivid images and recollections.

He recalled other "Things" that he had talked over with Jen.

Micah had no recollection of a childhood, because Micah had never had a childhood. Instead, he had the memories of a child who had been called "Ruby." Even these faded with every passing month and week, to the point where, for the most part, Micah often couldn't remember if he was remembering something that had happened to Ruby or something he had read in a book at some point. But one thing remained clear: the First Thing. With Ruby's older sister and brother looking on, excited and confused, Ruby's mother red-faced and enraged, Ruby, with clenched fists, had said that she would not wear the dress. A class mate at her school, a girl who Ruby interacted with little and liked less, had invited all the girls in the class to her tenth birthday party. The party was to have a "princess theme." All the girls were expected to come dressed as princesses and be introduced at the door by their royal princess titles.

For Ruby's mother, struggling to raise three children alone with a series of low-paying jobs, this dress had been an extravagance. She was wondering how she would pay for gas in the coming week to get herself to and from her job cleaning the local hospital. And here was her youngest child, secretly her favorite, refusing to put on the dress (forty dollars!) that she had bought for her.

"Then you don't get to go to the party!" her mother had yelled with frustration.

"Fine! I don't want to go to the stupid party! I don't want to wear that stupid dress!"

"Then you'll sit in your room all weekend! No books, no television."

"Fine!" Ruby had answered.

During that weekend Ruby had kept busy. She had sorted through all her clothes. No dresses. Nothing pink. Nothing pretty. And all her few belongings. The troll doll with the grape colored hair could stay. The troll doll with the yellow hair and the lipstick had to go. After kissing the doll goodbye, Ruby tossed it in the trash pile.

Ruby's mother admitted defeat. Ruby heard her crying. But the trash pile was taken to Goodwill for donation.

Because Ruby knew that she had hurt her mother, and had hurt her by being something rather than by doing something, she promised herself that she would from then on do whatever she could to make her mother happy. Ruby, serious and intelligent, had applied herself to her school work. Report card after report card was all A's. This brought tears of joy and hugs that seemed to last forever from her mother. "I'm so proud of you!" her mother said, and beamed with genuine pride at Ruby in her baggy jeans, oversized San Diego Chargers jersey, and short hair underneath her backwards baseball cap. "You'll be able to do anything you want when you grow up!"

With her grades and her extracurricular activities (captain of her high school girls' lacrosse team, editor of the school paper), the first "anything" was a full academic scholarship to the University of California at San Diego.

That was where the second Thing happened. As a freshman with an undeclared major, mostly bored with courses which the other students seemed to find so difficult, walking across campus Ruby had first set her eyes on Faye Short, PhD. Doctor Short didn't walk — she strode. She affected the dress of an Oxford don (Doctor Short had done graduate work at Oxford) with her tweed jacket and wool pants.

"Who is that?" Ruby had asked. She found out that Faye Short was the head of the small but acclaimed Classics Department. Ruby declared her major the next day.

About the time she dropped Intro to Geology and started taking Latin I, Ruby made an appointment through the university behavioral health services. Ruby didn't know why she felt the way she did. "Shut down" was the best term she had to describe it. But she was aware that the people around her did not share this experience.

And so she had been paired with Jen. Jen and Doctor Short became the twin suns around which "Ruby" revolved, sometimes in a flattened ellipse, sometimes in a figure eight pattern. Doctor Short knew a brilliant academic mind when she came across one. She demanded the utmost from "Ruby." Jen knew, or thought she knew, a young woman coming to terms with being a lesbian. But quickly Jen saw that this was not correct. "Ruby" was not conflicted about her erotic desires for other women. "Ruby's" erotic desires were vague. Ruby much preferred the company of boys, and slowly, with Jen as a sounding board, realized that the great longing of her life was to experience the world not as "Ruby," but as a boy.

Micah thought of the two years that followed as the Not Yet Micah time. Not Yet Micah, as Faye Short's star student, didn't have much time for contemplation. Micah had come upon her slowly. In the abandoned Intro to Geology class she had come across mica, a mineral, once used to make window panes. A piece of mica is called a book because it is almost infinitely separable into finer and finer sheets, almost down to the molecular level. "Ruby" became Micah, trading one mineral name for another.

Micah drifted towards the Trans/Queer group on campus, and barely made it in the door when he was set upon by Eleanor. Eleanor was tall, femme, and whipsmart, offering incisive analyses of gender oppression in its many hydra-headed manifestations.

With Eleanor at his side, Micah encountered the next Thing. Attending an LGBTQ arts festival, Micah and Eleanor surveyed items on offer in a silent auction. Micah found the book. It was a beautifully bound coffee table book, a compendium of the works of Tom of Finland. Micah was enraptured. Here were beautifully-done drawings of men, impossibly masculine men, butting up against each other like young rams; but the contest was not to determine which would couple with a ewe, it was to determine who would sexually submit to whom. And all this, Micah noticed, depicted in broad daylight. No shame and no tentativeness for these men. Over his shoulder, if he had been listening, he would have heard Eleanor dismiss the book as "patriarchal bullshit," but Micah didn't hear Eleanor and, in fact, never really heard another thing that Eleanor said again. When the winners of the silent auction were declared, Micah put the book on his "only for emergencies" credit card and was still holding it close to his chest, walking away, when he saw a man dressed just like those drawings in the book.

So. These men existed not just in the mind of Tom of Finland, but were out here walking around in the world. Micah introduced himself to the man and got an invitation to a meeting.

When Micah reported about this latest Thing to Jen, Jen felt herself for the first time in her therapeutic relationship with Micah to be out of her depth. She asked around and found a referral to a colleague, a highly regarded clinical psychologist and psychotherapist who was also "in that community" and whose practice largely served members of that community.

In alternating weeks Micah started to see both Jen and Lewis Shaughnessy, D.Sc. And, because of the invitation of Stewart, the man he had met that day at the LGBTQ arts festival, Micah entered the world of the San Diego leather community.

This community came to mean so much to him that after graduation, with honors, he broke Doctor Short's heart and decided to wait before going further into academia. Doctor Short, undaunted, had activated the San Diego cell of the International Underground Lesbian Revolutionary Conspiracy and found for her pupil a job she felt sure would leave him very soon pounding on the door, begging to be readmitted, to the Ivory Tower of Academe. Micah started work as a veterinary technician at an animal hospital; the primary responsibility of this job was to clean up poop.

Meanwhile, his relationship with Doctor Shaughnessy grew into a friendship and mentorship. He became "Lew" to Micah.

And so it was that Micah was invited to a private party at Lew's home. "I have a dungeon," he told her, "and most of the men there will end up in the dungeon after dinner and cigars, but you can see how that goes for you."

Dinner was excellent, served up by a team of men wearing only jockstraps and boots, some of whom Micah knew from leather community events. Micah listened much more than he contributed to conversation at the table, particularly to a man named Ryan, in town for the event with an older man named Ralph.

Ryan recounted the death of a man named Farley Lustig. When he talked about that day in the desert outside of Borrego Springs, Micah held his breath as Lew and Ryan embraced, and Lew cried openly and without restraint.

After dinner most of the men left the deck overlooking the canyon, upon the slopes of which the house was built, to head to the dungeon. Some stayed behind, the man named Ryan among them. Micah fetched himself another beer and sat down in the empty chair next to Ryan. Ryan was preparing a cigar for smoking. He smiled at Micah and said he had another if Micah would like to enjoy one with him.

"This would be my first time," Micah answered.

Ryan was happy to initiate the handsome young man, thinking how good he would look hauling on a cigar. He patiently explained the basics — how the color of the rapper indicates the type of tobacco leaf that fills it: light-colored wrappers have tobacco aged for less time so that the taste had a quality called "grassy," which some people liked, but Ryan did not. His preference was for a dark brown "maduro" wrapper, which gave a strong, slightly bitter smoke. Cigars, he continued, are fragile. They can dry out and turn to un-smokable paper in a day if not stored with the proper humidity. Ryan demonstrated to Micah how to seal the wrapper by wetting his lips, putting it whole into his mouth, then drawing it out slowly, closing his spit-slicked lips gently around it, then twirling it between his palms. Micah followed suit.

Next came the cutting of the cigar. Ryan preferred to cut off the tip rather than punching a hole in the end.

Then the lighting. Holding a cigar in one hand and a lit wooden match in the other, Ryan "toasted" the end. Then, putting the cigar in his mouth, he applied the match, puffing gently and rotating the cigar slowly until a nice, even cherry formed at the end. Ryan, a lifelong smoker, told Micah that he liked letting his lungs slowly fill with the thick smoke, which required practice and application, but if Micah just decided to "sip" the smoke, holding it in his mouth and letting the smoke slowly drift out, there was no shame in that.

"To smoke a cigar is to understand connoisseurship," Ryan concluded before Micah lit his cigar. "As you light it, notice the flavor. That will change as you smoke, different notes suggesting different tastes and experiences—coffee, brandy, burnt sugar—may emerge. And towards the finish, as the cigar burns down, new flavors will emerge and come to predominate. All of which should be appreciated."

"So it's like a journey," said Micah.

"Just like that," said Ryan nodding.

Micah lit his cigar. Ryan's dick swelled. Here was this handsome boy, undertaking a practice often part of an initiation into manhood, and under Ryan's tutelage.

Micah at first felt slightly dizzy with the the first draw on the cigar, then warm and alert, not just to the experience, but to the man sitting next to him. The mustache on his face, full and lush, was that pale straw color that men who were blond in their youth take on as they age. His thick, untrimmed eyebrows were the same color, over blue eyes that made the adjective "laughing" appropriate. "He has such a kind face," thought Micah.

"So tell me about your journey," said Ryan.

Micah started off with the Tom of Finland book. He talked about the San Diego leather community, the experiences he had had, the pup moshes, the muscular marine who had told him that at home with his Daddy he was a "little," about three years old, the recent demonstration of temporary piercing he had attended, watching as a professional Domme turned her submissive into a porcupine with long acupuncture needles.

Micah noticed that Ryan's blue eyes had a faraway look in them. "I guess things were pretty different when you were my age," he said.

"They were," said Ryan. "It was a secret thing. Men often sought it out in desperation. And once you found it, there was a sense that in doing so you had separated yourself from the world you had left behind. Although you didn't miss it much.

"I think of myself as a Twentieth-Century Leatherman. It was in the last century that I had experiences that were powerful, that changed me completely in the course of one night. And I had those experiences with men..." (Ryan paused and swallowed hard) "...men the likes of which I don't think we shall see again once the few who remain are no longer among us."

Ryan turned and looked at Lew, Ralph, and a few of the older men, sitting together speaking quietly under a cloud of pipe and cigar smoke that hung over them in the still evening air.

"Leather contests make me sad," Ryan continued. "They make me feel as though all we have now is a kind of museum. We dust off the relics that are on exhibit there, but we have forgotten their meaning. And the power that they once had. I wish that it could somehow be preserved, but I don't see how. All things come and go out of existence, I guess. I wish this one didn't have to."

"The Rites of the Cult of Mithras," said Micah.

Ryan gave him a blank look, but Micah was used to that. Micah had done his senior independent research project on the Mithraic cults. It was his greatest enthusiasm.

Micah explained that in the third and fourth century of the Common Era, Christianity was really taking off. Throughout the Roman Empire, and even in Rome itself, the new religion was gaining more and more adherents, reaching into the upper echelons of Roman society. The wives of Senators and Centurions in particular were extremely susceptible to the Hebrew Messiah. Their husbands were much slower to adopt the new beliefs. Indeed, the Roman values of valor and strength seemed wholly at odds with the new virtues of meekness and mildness. And so the men started meeting in secret. They built underground bunkers where they would gather. They adopted an obscure myth from the East as their own and devised a gnostic scheme of rites, raising initiates through greater and greater esteem among their fellows, the summit of which was *Pater*, or Father.

Now Micah looked at the circle of older leathermen smoking, sitting in their deck chairs, talking quietly, enjoying a bottle of single malt Scotch whiskey their host had provided.

"We don't know much about their beliefs," Micah continued. He paused to draw on his cigar. To his own surprise the draw was deep; he felt the warmth of the smoke sink into his lungs. Then he slowly exhaled. "That's very likely because they didn't have any. But what we do know is what they did when they were together. They would feast and get drunk. In Mithraic temples which have been found, as far north as England, ground is littered with beef bones, apple cores, the residue of wine. Those men had a great time together while their women went off to church."

Ryan regarded Micah with new admiration. Micah saw that behind his face wheels were turning.

"How would you feel, boy, if we went downstairs and engaged in a rite of our own."

Although Micah had never been addressed as "boy" before, he barely noticed.

"I would like that, Sir," he answered.

Downstairs in the dungeon, Ryan took off Micah's leather jacket and leather uniform shirt, stripping him to the waist. They found a space in the now crowded and busy dungeon where an overhead joist in the roof offered an eye bolt. Ryan dug a pair of wrist restraints from the black duffle bag he had brought with him. Micah offered his outstretched arms to Ryan. Ryan buckled on the restraints. He used a quick-release snap used in mountaineering to attach a length of chain to the eye bolt, and to this he padlocked the the wrist restraints Micah now wore. As each padlock clicked into place he looked at Micah, drawing his gaze and attention, before driving the lock home so that Micah distinctly heard the "click." Ryan smiled as he watched Micah's face betray the implications of the padlock settling with the young man.

Next Ryan put in place a white plastic mouthguard. Micah gagged slightly as it was forced into his mouth. He started salivating, the drool dripping from the corners of his mouth.

Ryan turned his back, digging in the duffle bag, then seemed to find what he was looking for. He fumbled with something, then stood, and walking away from Micah, got the attention of a man watching a flogging scene. The man nodded, and, with Ryan's back to Micah, they seemed to be fumbling with something Micah could not see.

When Ryan turned to face Micah he was wearing a pair of black boxing gloves. The man had laced him into them. After punching the gloves together a few times, Ryan began circling Micah, making a few initial tentative jabs to Micah's chest and torso, dancing like a boxer as he did so. A blow to Micah's chest was stronger than those that preceded it. For an instant Micah was winded. "Keep breathing," Ryan barked. "Don't hold your breath. Let your muscles be supple. Just take the punch."

Micah did as he was told. He kept his eyes looking into Ryan's. Ryan was smiling. "He's enjoying himself," thought Micah. And Micah realized that he was enjoying himself, too. He liked showing the man that he could take it, his eyes and his vocalizations made unintelligible by the mouthguard daring him to deliver more. Ryan delivered more.

After pummeling Micah's torso, Ryan bent his head close to that of the young man. "Now, boy, I want you to tighten up your abdominals. Make them rock hard."

Micah did so. Ryan, maintaining eye contact, his face inches from Micah's, gave a quick one-two punch. Then another. Then another. Then a series in quick succession. The blows felt like slaps, but Micah, clenching his midriff, felt the burning that comes with muscle fatigue. It was to be a duel between Ryan's punches and Micah's ability to hold his abdominals taut. Ryan continued the rabbit punches, as they continued to stare into each other's eyes. Ryan made a growling noise at the back of his throat. Micah responded with his own defiant growl. Micah's belly was now on fire, the muscles screamed to relax, but Micah knew if he allowed them to go soft for a second, any blow that fell would knock the wind out of him. Micah willed his exhausted muscles to continue the agony of the resistance to Ryan's punches, both of them doing the call and response of louder and louder animalistic growls.

Then Ryan ceased. He took a half step backwards. With one gloved hand he caressed Micah's cheek. "Very good, boy," he said, "very good indeed."

Micah relaxed. As he did so, Ryan caught the boy's jaw with a slow, glancing punch from his free hand, taking his glove away from Ryan's face. Micah saw stars. And his adrenaline kicked in.

Micah was reminded of the days and weeks after he started administering to himself shots of testosterone. Suddenly the go-along-to-get-along person he had been was gone forever. A stolen parking space had him bolting from his car, everything a dark red haze except the face of an insolent teenage boy emerging from his own car. The boy fled. Micah kicked at the tires of the boy's car, called "Fuck you, asshole!" after him, and gave a "Fuck you, too!" to the driver behind Micah's idling car sitting in the middle of the lane.

"Uhhh!" was all Micah could muster with the mouthguard in place. Ryan placed a few more punches on Micah's jaw. Micah's breathing became labored. He jerked his arms against the restraints and chain. He tried to deliver a knee to Ryan's groin, which Ryan neatly avoided and rewarded Micah with another punch to the jaw.

Then Ryan stepped next to Micah. Micah glared at him with rage. Ryan whispered in Micah's ear, "What are they going to say at work on Monday morning when you show up with a black eye?"

The shock on the face of his co-workers, the looks of concern flashed through Micah's head.

"You can tell them you got in a fight," said Ryan. "'Yeah, but you should see the other guy,' you can say. You brawler. Mister Tough Guy. You want that, Tough Guy? You want a nice shiner to wear around for a few days? You want a Reputation as a man not to be fucked with? How about it, boy? Want that shiner?"

Micah nodded.

Ryan knew exactly what he was doing. Years ago, back in the GMSMA days, he had been introduced to a man at the periphery of the leather world. A man who was viewed somewhat with suspicion by many. He went by the name of "punchpig." Punching scenes were what he was all about. Nothing else. "How'd you like to get punched in the face sometime?" was punchpig's opener to Ryan. Ryan would have had to think long and hard to come up with a list of ten things he wanted less.

But punchpig had set his sites on Ryan. They would meet for coffee. punchpig would tell him about the dynamics of the scene, about how it wasn't the power of the blow if they were talking about face punching; it was more a series of surgical strikes. It didn't take much to give a man a fat lip or a bloody nose. Or a black eye. "A few well placed jabs to the occipital lobe is enough for a black eye," he had explained smiling.

And with regularity Ryan would find emails from punchpig. The subject was always the same: "for you, punchmeat" and the only content would be of men boxing. Often without knowing the sender and the context, Ryan would have taken the pictures as stills from gay porn. The expressions on the men's faces were intense and aroused. In addition to the action shots there were photos of boxers after the fight, smiling or looking defeated, with fat lips, bloody noses, and black eyes. Ryan found those images cropping up in his jerk-off fantasies, those powerful men, their power and grit evident on their faces. Win or lose, they had prevailed.

Finally Ryan had sent a simple reply: when and where?

punchpig had come to him, to his studio apartment on Stanton Street. First, being all buddy-buddy, he had put Ryan in wrist-thigh restraints. Then, his voice in soothing hypnotic tones, he had put on the sparring gloves. And then it started.

In anticipation he remembered what punchpig had said about quick, light little jabs. He imagined himself being hard and stoic, muscling his way through it. How bad could it be?

What Ryan did not realize was that even experienced boxers flinch from a blow to the face. Instinctively. Your head is where your brain is. You could lose a limb and still survive, but a blow to the head and it could be all over for you. And when you are unable to put up your dukes to either defend or protect yourself, adrenaline, the neurochemical that triggers the "fight or flight" response, starts pumping into your bloodstream. But Ryan, who could neither fight nor flee, very quickly was burying his face in the rug by his bed, screaming and crying. punchpig offered more soothing words, calming Ryan, and then let go with another jab. But then it happened.

Still screaming, still crying, Ryan was aware on a fundamental level that he would come through this. There would be an After. And he knew this because he sensed the empathy and the decency of the man who was punching him in the face. He would be okay.

punchpig continued until he stopped. Ryan's breathing and heart rate slowly, very slowly, returned to normal. In the aftermath of the adrenaline rush he was buoyant and giggling. Still in the restraints, punchpig had led him to the bathroom and showed him himself in the mirror. Around his right eye it was red and swollen. punchpig had also raised a swollen lump, which he called a "mouse" on his left cheekbone. As they talked he released Ryan from his restraints, talked some more, while the right eye continued to swell, and the swell around the slit turned from red to dark purple.

They had headed to a coffee place on Eighth Avenue with big comfy chairs. punchpig treated Ryan to a latte. While he was ordering, Ryan realized that as he looked around the room, he met no one's eyes. They were all staring but were careful to avoid meeting his gaze. Ryan was the dangerous one. The unknown element. The guy with the shiner.

As they sipped their hot coffee, punchpig told Ryan that he wanted to return the favor. He talked Ryan through the finer points of technique, demonstrated on an egg-shaped pillow with a face drawn on it, and then watched and gave notes as Ryan put on the gloves. punchpig had decided that Ryan was ready, and Ryan had for the first but not the last time, the honor of punching punchpig.

"It's coming up really nice," Ryan said to Micah. He gently touched his right temple.

"Fuck, man, that was amazing!" was all Micah could repeat. "Fucking amazing!"

"You're one tough little thug, aren't you?"

Micah giggled and sipped the herbal tea that Ryan had found in Lew's kitchen and made for him.

"I'll tell you something else about yourself, tough little thug. You've got some boy in you, too."

Micah looked solemnly at Ryan.

"Yes, you do. You've got some boy in you."

Ryan and Micah wrapped their arms around each other and kissed.

"Yes, Sir," said Micah.

"You know what else, boy? You've got some slave in you. Somewhere deep, deep down. Very deep down. There's a part of you that wants to be a man's property. You might not realize it yet, but I know it's there."

Ryan said, "I'd like for you to come next Friday and stay with me for a weekend in Palm Springs. Could you do that?"

Micah remembered that he had on his schedule a Florentine flogging workshop the following Saturday afternoon.

"I could do that, Sir."

"Good boy," said Ryan.

Later that night, lying in bed, her two housemates so absorbed in the online role-play game they were playing they hadn't even looked up when he came in, Micah was ecstatic. He felt he had connected with some dark, ancient power. He imagined himself walking in Ryan's footsteps as the older man, clad in a toga, led him through a desolate nighttime district on the outskirts of Rome. They came to a what looked like a mausoleum, sealed with an iron door. Ryan rapped a tattoo on the door. There was a series of knocks in answer, and another reply from Ryan. Slowly the door creaked open. "*Salve!*" said the man behind the door in greeting. "*Salve!*" answered Ryan and Micah in unison.

Through the door was a flight of stairs leading down into the earth. At the bottom the faint glow of torchlight and the murmur of men's voices. At the foot of the stairs was a small antechamber. More greetings. Ryan and Micah gave over their cloaks and togas, which were accepted by one of the men with a bow. Then they proceeded through another door, this one of wood. Ryan pushed open the door. Over Ryan's shoulder Micah saw a long table, benches on either side. About a dozen men sat on benches on each side, shouting down the table. The table was loaded with vessels and patens with all manner of food. At the head of the table sat a fat old satyr of a man. As Ryan stepped forward into the room, Micah following, the men fell silent.

"Ryan! *Salve!*" said the man at the head of the table.

"I present to you all my slave, Micah!" answered Ryan in Latin.

"*Salve* Micah!" the men bellowed in unison.

"You are not a slave here, Micah," said the man at the head of the table, "We are all of us brothers, and we welcome you as a brother!" He continued, laughing heartily, "Except for me. I am *Pater*. Make room for your new brother, my sons!"

Naked.

The reverie ended. Naked.

Micah reached over and grabbed his phone from the charger.

Choosing his words carefully, he composed an email to Ryan. Micah explained he was a man, but he was different from other men. He explained as briefly as he could how he was different. "I'll understand, Sir, if you want to rescind your invitation, knowing what you now know about me, Sir."

With his finger trembling, he tapped the arrow that sent the email to Ryan.

Micah drew the covers around him.

He began to recite a prayer to Mercury, whom he thought of as his protector, that he had learned his second semester. Halfway through the prayer, his phone gave a little chirp. Ryan had sent him a text message. "What time can you be here on Friday, boy?"

The silent parade of images through Micah's mind slowed. He hung motionless in the bondage suit. Before his thoughts melted into dark gray oblivion, he thought of a chrysalis. What would propel the larva to seal itself away like that. As being a grub or caterpillar had been the only existence it had ever known, it must be beyond the reckoning or imagination—not that larvae were capable of either—to do so in order to obtain a new way of being. But there it would be until the Parousia, the Fullness of Time. When the possibilities of the past life were exhausted, when all the tastes had been tasted, all the sights seen, all the music heard, when the sea of emotions that had carried it along had dried up, then it was time for a new existence, a new way of being. Something that the the vanishing self could never imagine. Chrysalis. Parousia. Greek words.

Micah had found learning Latin easy, as though he had heard it spoken in the cradle but through some quirk of fate had been taught English. Greek was another thing altogether. Greek had been a frustrating undertaking. Even after years of diligent study Micah did not trust that what he expressed in Greek was what was being conveyed. But Greek was a language of words that were like doorways. You did not throw down a word like a playing card as you did in English. "Hot" or "Cold" or "Hard" or "Easy." Greek words were filled with nuance. You had to go to the context, then to the speaker, then to the situation, and see a tiny glimmer of what was being suggested.

Chrysalis. His black, leather chrysalis. He wondered as what he would emerge. What new form of life would emerge from the second skin once the buckles were removed.

Sitting a little way away, careful not to make the slightest noise, half reclining in the leather club chair that had belonged to his Master and now belonged to him, Ryan wondered the same thing. But he had hopes, or rather, one specific hope, about what form this new creature would take. It would be his and his completely.

Afterword

I sing a song of the saints of God,
Patient brave and true,
Who toiled and fought and lived and died
For the Lord they loved and knew.

. . .

And one was a soldier, and one was a priest,
And one was slain by a fierce wild beast:
And there's not any reason, no, not the least,
Why I shouldn't be one too.

Lesbia Scott, *The Hymnal of the Protestant Episcopal Church in the United States of America 1940, #243.*

So I sang in Sunday school and I took the words very much to heart. All of us by baptism are called to be good Christians, to love and serve God and our neighbor, but for some of us that means a life of trial, tribulation, and ultimate triumph to such a degree that our images are preserved in stained glass to inspire the faithful. And, one year for my birthday, I received a book: *D'Aulaires' Book of Greek Myths*. In it I read about Jason, Orpheus, Odysseus, and Heracles, heroes marked by the gods to live extraordinary lives of adventure. That was what I wanted: an extraordinary life of adventure. I wanted to be tested. I wanted to contend with monsters and prevail. I wanted to descend into Hell itself and re-emerge.

This was very unlikely. My father was a food inspector for the Pennsylvania Department of Agriculture. My mother was an immigrant from Scotland. We lived in Bucks County, Pennsylvania, where the cows outnumbered the people. The nearest town was eight miles away. The world was free of monsters. In my explorations of the uncharted (by me) wilderness behind my house I only saw pheasants and white-tailed deer.

All that changed when puberty hit. One day I was sprawled on the floor playing with my plastic dinosaurs, the next day I was stalking the men who stopped the garbage truck at the end of our driveway and collected our trash, jumping at every opportunity to go "into town," for an oil change to the Dodge, and, especially, to go with my father to the barber to get a hair cut. Every opportunity to see men, men being men, men relating to other men, men talking to other men the way men talked to other men . . . I wanted that.

When I realized that I was a attracted to men, I did not have much of a struggle in accepting this. In fact, I welcomed it. I have a clear recollection of seeing a commercial for toothpaste: mom and two kids come home after a trip to the dentist and announce to dad that they have no cavities. I remember being aware that the people and the scenario presented in the commercial — the sunny, suburban living room, the nuclear family — would not be my life. My life was going to be something that I could not then imagine.

When I was sixteen, I got my driver's license and I got a job washing dishes at a restaurant down in New Hope, a small town on the banks of the Delaware River. New Hope had been a weekend getaway for Dorothy Parker, George S. Kaufman, and the other members of the Algonquin Round Table. In the 1940s and 1950s, it was an artists' colony of sorts. When Richard Rogers wrote about the "corn is as high as an elephant's eye" in the musical *Oklahoma!*, he was looking out on a Bucks County corn field. In the 1960s and 1970s, the hippies came in, and with them came a surprising number of gay men and lesbians. That little town was home to three gay bars, the New Prelude, the Cartwheel, and the Raven.

Working in the kitchen of Mother's Restaurant, I got to meet and know adult gay men who were relatively happy and well adjusted and were not lonely, tragic figures destined for suicide or violent death as were the gay men on television and in movies.

But more importantly, I made the discovery that after dark, along the banks of the canal that went through town, men would walk the towpath looking for sex with each other.

This was my first taste of adventure. In pitch black midnight I would survey the night's fellow strollers, approach or be approached, and get my dick sucked. On occasion, we had to run from the cops. I heard rare reports of men being beaten and robbed. There was danger in the darkness. Every visit was a heart-pounding exhilaration.

Long before I knew I was gay I knew that for me, scenarios where one man was in charge and the other man was very much not in charge were powerfully erotic. Although I had little struggle accepting my same-sex attraction, this other element concerned me greatly. I didn't sense this in the adult gay men that I knew and believed that this would make me an outcast among outcasts, perhaps unique.

Then a miracle happened. The summer before I went off to college, I found and read through a stack of *Drummer* magazines. Far from being the only one, we were legion. We had bars and clubs and even had a magazine. All I had to do was bide my time and my extraordinary life, filled with adventure, would begin.

There was another element in the background that would make my life extraordinary as well. On July 3, 1981, a few months after I started my nighttime perambulations along the towpath, an article in the *New York Times* carried the headline "Rare Cancer Seen in 41 Homosexuals." My sexual experiences dovetailed almost exactly to the AIDS crisis. Indeed there would be monsters in my heroic life, and a descent into Hades.

Forty years later, here I sit in my living room in Palm Springs. My life has indeed been extraordinary. Legendary leathermen have been my friends and mentors. I have survived ordeals that would have crushed other men (and collapsed crying and grateful afterwards into the arms of the men who meted out those ordeals). If the experience of me throwing my bullwhip at the back of the man stretched out on the cross before me and hearing the resounding crack differs much from what Zeus felt hurling a thunderbolt, I can't imagine how or to what degree. Life, death, courage, compassion, ecstasy, desolation . . . . I have compassed these many times, sometimes all in a single weekend.

A common occurrence for me: I tell a story, one of my many stories ("At my first Inferno . . .") and my listener tells me, "You need to write a book." During the early months of the COVID lockdown, when we were all encouraged to stay home and not leave unless it was absolutely necessary, I had the time and opportunity to do just that. And also, as the world was brought to a halt by a global pandemic, my memories of another earlier pandemic were first faint echoes and then came rushing back with clarity. And so I wrote that book. Rather than put it in the form of a memoire, I decided to fictionalize it. I am Farley. I am Ryan. I am, in part, Micah. Their experiences are for the most part my experiences. Their reflections and insights are mine as well. The other characters are real people, too. I will neither confirm nor deny any fictional and real life parallels because had I included all the people I ought to have included, who have shaped the man I am to some degree, it would not be a book but a series, and lockdown is over and my schedule is filling up once again.

To the extent I had a purpose in writing this book, it is to cleave asunder a Gordian knot that has been with us for too long. I first encountered the term "Old Guard Leatherman" in chat rooms on AOL in the 1990s, typically in the profiles of Masters seeking slaves to serve them without limits or cessation on a "24/7/365" basis. These were the early days of the internet; we were all finding our way through that *Midsummer Night's Dream* forest. Also, we were still in the throes of the AIDS crisis. Although the term was not used then, we were cat-fishing each other. How better to establish *bona fides* in the few words available in your profile than to allude to a fantasy world drawn from the fiction of John Preston and others? The worst that ever came from all that intrigue was disappointment when rather than abducting you into chattel slavery NYCMaster4slave deletes his screen name and disappears into the ether.

Unfortunately, the Old Guard idea has metastasized into something pernicious and is still bandied about. In and of itself it is a relatively harmless bid for borrowed glory and authenticity, more to be pitied than scorned. That said, it carries implications of a regimented, ordered underground, like KAOS that Maxwell Smart and 99 dealt with on *Get Smart*. This is pernicious because it replaces with fiction and fantasy a glorious and wonderful history.

Imagine that it is the year 1935. You are twenty-five years old. You are a homosexual. Your life is going to be one of misery, terror, and loneliness. To let anyone know of your dark and terrible secret means the end of everything.

Now imagine that the year is 1950. Again, you are twenty-five years old and you are a homosexual. You served your country in the War, plucked from the little town where you grew up in Indiana, Wisconsin, Alabama, or Idaho, and in basic training and on troop ships and in barracks, you made the discovery that you were not "the only one," not by a long shot. Now, the war is over. Rather than going back home to the farm, you have decided to stay in the city where you were discharged, Los Angeles. With no need for all the motorcycles used by couriers during the war, the military is selling them cheap and you buy one. In 1950, Los Angeles was a city of only four million people. The freeways had yet to be built. Getting from downtown LA out to Long Beach on your motorcycle took the better part of an afternoon as you rode through orange groves. One day you stop at a road house to wash the dust from your throat with a cold beer. As you park your bike, another young man your age rides up on his motorcycle. You look at him. He looks at you. You both know everything you need to know about each other.

The Nineteen Fifties was an era of hyper-conformity and McCarthyism. A homosexual's life could be destroyed with an anonymous letter sent to his boss or to the local chief of police. He would lose everything: his job, his home, his life. But during that time, those men on motorcycles, leathered up like Marlon Brando in *The Wild One*, not only were able to find each other but to trust each other with their names and their lives. They built a community and found a way to live rich and wonderful lives full of love and laughter and fellowship.

Things got better for some gay men during the 1960s, and in the last year of that decade, the Stonewall Uprising changed everything. But other gay men, whose erotic lives centered around games of power and ordeals of pain, were still outcasts among outcasts. Homosexuality would be excised as a disorder from the psychiatrist's *Diagnostic and Statistical Manual* but Sado-Masochism would remain for decades. It was sick and deviant and dangerous. But by using a complex system of codes organically developed, mostly involving a lot of cow hide, these men were also able to find each other and in spite of the best efforts of a hostile world and live lives filled with love and fellowship.

And then, in the 1980s, a great evil arose. Gay men began to die by the hundreds and then the thousands. When there was an outbreak of what came to be called Legionnaire's Disease at the Bellevue-Stratford Hotel in Philadelphia in 1976, the public health apparatus mobilized a response. Three years into the AIDS crisis, the federal government did not spend as much money fighting AIDS as it had fighting Legionnaire's Disease. In our time of need, the government, the medical and public health establishment, and the social services bureaucracy turned their collective back on us. For the first years of the epidemic, we were on our own. We had to build from the ground up an infrastructure to provide care and advocacy for gay men dying of AIDS.

In 1980, between Boston and Northern Virginia, there were over a thousand leather community clubs and organizations, and these clubs proliferated in other parts of the country, too. There was a tradition among the motorcycle clubs that when one of their members had a spill on his bike, was in the hospital, couldn't work, the hat would be passed and a collection would be taken. Each of those hundreds of clubs had a treasurer and a bank account and knew how to raise money. With gay men dying and money desperately needed for these new organizations — Gay Men's Health Crisis, AIDS Project Los Angeles, the Shanti Project — leather clubs did what they had always done: they raised money to help their brothers. (In the early years, and still today, even in the wider gay community, stigma attached itself to leather. Often, these donations would go unacknowledged by the beneficiaries for fear that it would dampen the enthusiasm for the cause of other donors.)

And so you see, Twentieth-Century Leathermen are Jason and the Argonauts, Odysseus and his crew, Saint Ignatius of Loyola and his Soldiers for Christ, the Jesuits. We banded together, an army of lovers, we set off for adventure in a dangerous world relying only on our courage and on each other.

Our story — and *our stories* — need to be told. This book is my
humble attempt to do so.